KIM HARNES

Evernight Teen

www.evernightteen.com

STILL PHOTO

Copyright© 2014 Kim Harnes

ISBN: 978-1-77130-767-3

Cover Artist: Sour Cherry Designs

Editor: JC Chute

KIM HARNES

DEDICATION

This book wouldn't have come to be without the help of many people.

Thank you to Ellen Hopkins and Suzanne Morgan Williams who introduced me to the Nevada chapter of the SCBWI, which, in turn, introduced me to so many people on the same path as I.

To Heather Petty, words can't express my thanks to you. What you have taught me about this industry, about writing, about getting past my own self-imposed limitations, is immeasurable. If you only knew the depths of my admiration and gratitude…

To my amazing agent Pam Van Hylckama Vlieg and Foreword Literary, thanks for believing in me and my work. I'm certainly looking forward to a lasting relationship.

To my writing/critique partners Dawn Callahan, Temoca Dixon, Huston Piner, Carolyn Wright, Julie Dillard, Tracy Clark, Chris Ledbetter, Naomi Canale, Nikki Mann—through countess Friday Night Write sessions, Word Wars, wine, laughs, and tears, thank you for encouraging me, helping me along, and pushing me to continue even when I didn't think I could.

A special thank you to the three teachers I had growing up who always encouraged me to write: Beverly Kichenmaster, Larry Tinsley, and Kim Rowlett. Please know you all made a difference in my life.

To my family, Sean, Kyndra, Katie, and Sierra, who endured innumerable writes and rewrites, and who only rolled their eyes sometimes when I'd ask, "How about this?" and, "Do you like it better this way or that way?" and, "Well, what if I tried this?" And to Taryn, who wouldn't allow me to include her in with my family only because she'd rather hold the title of my Biggest Fan.

I know I've forgotten some, and don't have room to say thank you to so many more! You know who you are. Thank you.

STILL PHOTO

Kim Harnes

Copyright © 2014

Within us all lurks something dark,
the opposite of what we portray ourselves to be:
The yang to the yin,
the Ego to the Id—
the negative to the photograph...

Chapter One

Skinny women in butt floss.

That's what her boss had her photograph day in and day out.

Jess Waterford often wondered how women could wear thong underwear. They consisted of barely a half-centimeter of material to cover the front, after all, and a piece of thread in the back that was completely concealed by butt crack, which she surmised had to be ridiculously uncomfortable. Jess immediately and indiscreetly yanked out her underwear when they snuck northward to begin with. She certainly wasn't going to put anything there on purpose.

They also reminded her of her deadbeat mother, who had worn them constantly—usually with not much else. Her mother had been a model, and, unfortunately, had worn very little around the house. She had explained to Jess at a very young age that not only did it turn on her father, but it also showed off the stretch marks she blamed Jess for, and never let her forget. Almost daily reminders, actually, in black and blue shapes of whatever she'd had on hand to hit her with. Jess was overjoyed when, just days after her ninth birthday, her mother had taken off. And seven years later, she still didn't miss having her around.

"Are you ready?" George's gruff voice reminded her of where she was and her grip tightened on the camera strap.

Despite his preference in job assignments and his subjects' costumes, or lack thereof, George Caldwell was a great guy to work for. Jess had learned so much from him since she'd been his assistant at Starlight Fashion Magazine, and knew he'd provide the tools and knowledge she'd need to be able to hold her own as a photographer.

"Turn to the left, Angie," he said to the anorexic girl against the backdrop. "Arch your back and tilt your head to the side."

"But I can't move that way," Angie complained and stomped her foot tantrum-like, her high heel clicking on the floor, her silicone boobs bouncing stiffly in her bikini top.

George nudged Jess with his elbow in a watch-this gesture. "Well, if you can't move that way, there are seven other girls in the dressing room who can, and they're all waiting for their chance."

"Arch my back like this?"

He smiled. "And turn your head to the side."

"Like this?"

"Just like that." He turned back to Jess. "Threats usually work," he whispered and winked. His bushy, white eyebrow dipped with his eyelid.

She smiled back at him and began snapping pictures while he continued to direct Angie, each pose seemingly more complicated than the one prior. Jess wasn't sure exactly how a grown model would react to threats coming out of a sixteen-year-old girl with a borrowed camera and a voice like Minnie Mouse, so she was content with allowing George to be the bad guy—until he taught her how to threaten them properly, at least.

George adjusted a light and Jess stopped to change out a lens. "When do we get to start a project that actually piques *my* interest for a change?" She was thinking tall, dark, and handsome, of course. Torso with more ripples than Lake Tahoe on a breezy day. Abs like cement. She figured she could probably get used to staring at that.

"When I'm through with the projects that pique mine." George's eyes darted to each of Angie's assets.

"So, never then?" Jess knew defeat when she saw it, and went back to her work.

He chuckled. "The problem is this, Jess." He continued to talk to her while calling out commands to Angie. "You're only sixteen and (*Look sexy for me, Angie*) you can't go on location to shoot unless you have your father's approval. *(No, Angie, that doesn't look sexy, that looks constipated)*. If you can get him to sign the waivers, I can probably (*Pouty lips, now*) get you to come with us for the 'Men of Montego' spread in a few months."

"Montego?" Jess asked, standing up straight, all thoughts of Angie in a thong forgotten. "As in Montego Bay? As in Jamaica?"

"Do you know of a Montego Bay, North Dakota?"

"And you can get me the waivers today?"

He laughed at her eagerness. "How about I get approval first, and I'll have them for you by next week?"

"George," she said, her cheek muscles straining with the enormity of her smile, "you're the best."

"I don't do this for just anyone, you know."

"Um … hello?" an irritated voice beside them said. "Are you through with me? My ass is starting to cramp."

"Yes, Angie." George tried to stifle his laugh. "You can go get dressed now."

Jess looked at her watch. "Oh, shit! I have to go. I'm going to be late for school again." George was the only grown-up Jess knew who wasn't bothered by her use of profanity.

"See you Friday." He squeezed her shoulders. "Good work today."

Jess wanted to bask in the compliment but she didn't have time. She carefully loaded George's camera into its case and scrambled out the door, just barely making it to the stop in time to catch the bus to school.

Even though the pungent smell violated her nostrils as she stepped up, she beamed at the driver and paid her fare. Jess loved to ride the city bus. The diverse assortment of people who took public transportation amazed her, and she wished she could just take pictures of all of them to observe again and again. Today was no different. The driver herself was an obese woman whose backside overlapped the seat by several inches on each side. Her crisp, blue uniform shirt was impeccably clean, but Jess could tell the seams were straining at every stitch. Her taste in music was questionable, as well, and the sound of big bands invaded her ears. It was rather odd, she thought, for a forty-something black woman to like that stuff, and odder still to subject her passengers to it.

As she continued down the aisle, Jess eyed a tired-looking woman with two grocery bags and three children. The oldest child was holding the baby on her lap and Jess perceived the middle one had recently cried about something, because her eyes were red and there was dried snot caked around her nostrils.

A few rows behind them, a bald guy, covered in piercings and tattoos and apparently on some type of drug or another, rocked back and forth and punched the back of his seat as he barked obscenities.

Jess took a seat toward the back so she could observe the whole bus, and instantly became distracted by the young couple a few rows up that was only a thin layer of clothing away from having intercourse. She watched them until she almost missed her stop, and then blushed with embarrassment over her own voyeurism.

She exited the bus, taking one more glimpse of the romantic duo pressed against the window, and briskly walked the half block to school.

"Hi, Jess!" Brody met her by her locker and squeezed her around the waist. She was just about to tell him hello when he said, "How's my Muffin Top today?"

"You know," she retorted and pulled away, "I have enough of a complex about my weight from looking at Barbie dolls through a lens three days a week. I don't need it from you, too."

"You shouldn't have a complex, Babe. I've seen some of those girls in your magazine and all I can think about them is, 'Damn, Bitch! Eat a sandwich!'"

One of the things she loved most about Brody was that he always made her laugh. "Well, I could always start photographing other subjects."

"That might be a good idea."

"Really?" she asked coolly. "Even if that means I'm off to Jamaica for a couple weeks to photograph hot men in Speedos?"

He looked at her face to see if she was joking, and apparently realized she wasn't. "When are you going to Jamaica?" He looked down at the broken shoelace on his left sneaker.

"Maybe in a couple months." She put her hand on his chest and he looked back at her face. "George thinks he can get me in on a photo shoot there." Brody looked away again and Jess could feel his chest muscles become rigid beneath her palm. "It's a great opportunity, Brody. I'd learn a lot."

"What about school?" He averted her eyes and stared at the worn cover of his World Geography book, absentmindedly tracing over where he'd used his pocket knife to carve "Brody 'N Jess" in the bottom right corner. Jess took his change in demeanor to mean he didn't want her to go without him and he was already looking for lame excuses for her to stay, because he never gave a crap about school. His plan was to be a professional baseball player, and hers was to be a rich and famous photographer. With that as their future, who needed school?

"I can get my work ahead of time and bring it with me." She hadn't actually thought that far ahead since she'd just been told a half hour earlier. She was still trying to figure out how to persuade her over-protective single father to sign the waivers.

"Will you still call me?" He sounded hopeful, and finally looked her in the eyes.

She melted into the pools of silvery-blue that bored into her. "Every day." Jess wasn't usually an advocate for public displays of affection, but she was so overwhelmed by Brody's desire for her to stay with him. She put her arms around his neck, stood on her toes, and pressed her lips to his.

"Mmm." He glided his hand up and down her back as they parted. "What brought that on?"

She hugged his waist. "I just think it's really sweet that you don't want me to go."

He smiled. "I *really* don't want you to go." He leaned in to kiss her again.

Smiling at his newfound enthusiasm, she gently pushed him away as the bell rang. "Save it for later. We have to get to class."

Rejected, he kissed her cheek and turned away.

Jess, self proclaimed Queen of Observation, didn't fail to notice that he had his books held not at his side like usual, but in front of him as he strode to class.

He wants me, she thought, and smirked.

****

Brody spent most of the day with his sweatshirt in his lap while he was seated and his books in front of him as he walked. Every time he thought he might have a reprieve, his mind reverted back to the softness of Jess's lips, the feel of her fingers lightly brushing the nape of his neck, and the faint taste of spearmint toothpaste still on her tongue. He thought, more than once, that he might have to call a doctor like they advised to do on television, since his erection had clearly lasted longer than four hours. He also thought, more than once, that it was going to be completely impossible to squat behind the plate during baseball practice, let alone wear his cup. Would his teammates notice? The thought of certain ridicule in the locker room gave significant relief behind the zipper of his jeans and he began to feel better.

He wondered if Jess would show up to practice like she sometimes did when she didn't have to work in the afternoon. He really did love that girl. She had a fantastic smile. And beautiful eyes. A sweet voice. Perky boobs.

Brody grabbed his sweatshirt, put it back in his lap, and mumbled a few choice swear words under his breath.

"Do you have a problem, Mr. Campbell?" His science teacher Mr. Waller turned toward him, his back to the blackboard, chalk still in his hand.

Only a raging hard-on, Mr. Waller, he thought. "No." He shifted uncomfortably in his chair.

"Good. Then may I continue?"

He had already turned back around before Brody could respond.

Brody hated school and couldn't wait until graduation. He always knew he'd get into college on a baseball scholarship instead of grades. College wasn't for the continued education, of course, but for the chance to go pro. He was confident enough that he'd be in the Bigs in no time.

When the bell rang, Brody mentally checked his southern hemisphere, realized he could stand sans book, and headed toward the locker room for practice.

"'Sup, Brody?" Carter Benson socked him in the arm as he walked by.

"Hey, Carter. You haven't figured out how to change your shirt yet?" Brody laughed as Carter removed his blue t-shirt and slid on his jersey.

"Come on, man. You know this shirt makes me a chick magnet." Carter blushed through his dark skin and tossed the wadded up shirt into the bottom of his locker. "You gonna hit another homer against Spanish Springs tomorrow?"

"Hope so," Brody answered humbly and thumbed the combination on his locker. Though internally he knew he was that good, outwardly he didn't want to come off cocky and overconfident. He thought everyone would respect him more that way.

"Nah," Tom Hatter piped in. "It's a double header. Brody's gonna knock *three* outta the park."

Several of his teammates voiced their approval.

"There ain't a pitch thrown at Brody yet he can't hit," said the tall and slim Dave Towerey while pulling his mitt out of his locker.

"Yeah. That school home run record you got this year will never be broken. And you still have four games to add to it."

"Three home runs?" Carter asked Tom, sounding dubious. "Dude, you really are mad. Mad. As in Mad Hatter. Get it, 'cause your last name is Hatter?" He looked around the room and elbowed several players to make sure they heard him and awaited their response to his joke. None came, so he pretended to retie his cleat.

"Yeah, 'cause I haven't heard that one before, you Nimrod," Tom said sarcastically and threw a balled-up dirty sock in his face.

Brody smiled at his teammates' camaraderie, snatched up his gear, and took the field. When he got there Jason Boggs was already on the mound throwing to Coach Traynor. One of the things that made Brody a great catcher was the fact that Boggsie knew what he was doing when he pitched. They worked well together and fed off each other during games. Brody prided himself on knowing which pitch to call to make the batter swing, and Jason usually delivered it right where Brody put his mitt.

"Nice slider, Boggs." Brody strapped on his shin guards.

"Brody!" He turned toward the voice.

"Hey, Jess." He set the rest of his gear down and headed toward the chain link fence that separated them. "You staying for practice?"

"Of course."

The joy swirled within Brody. Just knowing she was there made him play better.

"But then Dad asked me to come straight home after that. Said he wanted to talk to me about something."

"Okay." He gripped the fence and absentmindedly kicked at the dirt with the toes of his cleats.

"I'll call you tonight and let you know what he said." She threaded her fingers through his.

He was pretty sure he knew her dad was going to say, "Stay away from Brody Campbell," since he'd just caught him in the process of trying to feel her up the day before. Wesley Waterford's timing was impeccable and he always broke up their best make out sessions.

Brody looked at their interlaced hands and took notice of the contrast against his skin—the hard, cold metal of the chain link and the soft, warm fingers of Jess's hand. When he looked back at her she was smiling her sideways smile that he loved so much. It was the smile that made only one cheek dimple and one eye squint. He felt his heart miss a beat, then pound hard as if trying to make up for it.

"Campbell!" Coach Traynor hollered, pulling him out of his trance. "You going to join the rest of us, or is Boggsie gonna pitch to you from the dugout?"

"Coming, Coach," Brody shouted back and then turned to Jess. "Talk to you tonight." He squeezed her hand, released it slowly, reluctantly, and then jogged over to home plate.

"I love you, Brody Campbell," she called after him.

The team took this as their chance to embarrass their captain as they wolf whistled and laughed. Those close enough swatted him with their mitts or slapped him on the back.

Brody felt his neck burn red.

KIM HARNES

Chapter Two

Brody brushed the dust off his pants and stood up straight.

"Nice slide, Campbell." Coach Traynor clapped his hands. "Let's call it a day, boys. Hit the showers."

Brody looked up in the stands and waved goodbye to Jess as she descended the bleachers. He was thankful he was already out of his catching gear. It meant he had more time to get to the locker room and let the shower rinse the ball field off his body. He'd only had a decent practice, mostly because of the nagging voice in the back of his head telling him he'd gotten Jess in trouble.

They had been friends since he was in the third grade. He was new to the school and a little on the shy side, and had taken the empty table closest to the door of the lunchroom. Content that no one had bothered with him, he'd sat there again the next day, and had an encounter he would never forget.

A dirty girl with a missing front tooth, lopsided pigtails, and gum on her face approached him and tossed a mostly empty brown sack on the table in front of him. "That's my spot," she said, noisily chomping the rest of the gum that had managed to make its way back into her mouth.

"I ... I ..." He stared at her, mouth open, shock freezing him to his seat.

"Did you hear me, butt hole?" She folded her arms in front of her.

Another girl stood from the table to his left. She was beautiful, prim and proper, her long red hair in a bow that matched her floral dress. "Leave him alone," she said, a little unsure of herself. "He sat there yesterday."

The messy girl yanked up her too-large jeans, the hole in the denim revealing the angry scrape on her knee. "But it's my seat and I wasn't here yesterday. I swallowed my tooth and my mom was scared I'd poop it out at school. See?" She stuck her pinky finger in the hole where her front tooth had been.

Brody just sat there between them, his tongue filling in his own new vacant space in his mouth from the tooth that had been knocked out at baseball practice, unsure of what to do.

"Well," the pretty girl said, "I think you should just let him stay there and you should find somewhere else. I don't like sitting next to you anyway."

"Well," the dirty girl retorted, "I think you should just move over by Henry Nose-Picker Pickering then, if you don't like sitting next to me, 'cause there's room at his table, too."

The pretty girl looked appalled. "I'm not moving."

The dirty girl blew a large bubble, popped it with her finger, and stuffed the wad back into her mouth. "I'm not moving either."

"Well, you have to now 'cause the new kid is in your seat." She didn't seem as pretty to Brody as she had before. Her lip was curled in a scowl making her nostrils flare, and her eye began to twitch.

The other girl, though unkempt in appearance, remained poised in attitude. "You know what my mom told me about girls that wear pantyhose?"

"What?" Her eyes inadvertently darted to the stockings on her legs.

"My mom said girls wear pantyhose to hold the stick in their butt."

The pretty girl pulled at the bow in her hair, knocking it askew. "Well, Jess Waterford, do you know what my mom told me about girls that play baseball?"

Brody's head snapped to the grimy girl to his right. "You play baseball?"

They'd been friends ever since.

Brody grinned at the memory as he watched her leave the field.

****

Jess wasn't exactly sure why her dad had asked her to come home right after Brody's practice. Her mind was abuzz with possibilities, initially thinking it may have been because she was late to school on Monday, followed by her getting caught making out with Brody when he'd brought her home on Tuesday. She also feared George had called and dropped the bomb about Jamaica. She had been pondering all day about how to break the news to her dad, and still hadn't come up with a plan. And, of course, most of all, she prayed upon all that was decent and holy that her mother hadn't returned. Bitch.

When she got to her house she took in a breath, prepared for the worst, and walked through the front door.

"Hi, Jess. How was school?" her dad asked as she entered the living room. He was in his favorite chair and looked relaxed enough. Jess's dad wasn't a large man, and certainly not scary, but he was stern. She knew he was struggling as a single father, and she tried hard not to disappoint him. At this point she wasn't sure if she had or not. She attempted to read his face, but his expression was blank.

"Fine," she answered. He sat up straight as she continued further into the room and Jess was suddenly consumed with the need to explode with apologies even though she wasn't sure what to apologize for. She was pretty sure she was about to find out.

"Have a seat." He gestured toward the couch.

She moved robotically and sat as she was told.

"Jess," he began, "there are a few things I want to talk to you about." His body language had changed again and Jess sensed nervous tension.

A few? "Okay." She swallowed hard.

"The office called to let me know you were late to school again on Monday."

"Yeah," she admitted. "I was rushing to finish at work and missed the bus. I had to wait fifteen minutes for the next one." Jess's mind was in a whirl. If he was pissed off about her being late to school because of work, he certainly wasn't going to let her miss two weeks to go to Jamaica.

"I know you love your job, Jess, but if it happens again, I'm going to have to rethink it," he said sternly. "Your education is very important to me. I know you think you've got your future all worked out, but you need the schooling to back it up, okay?"

"Okay." Agreement saves an argument, she thought.

He sighed deeply. "Now, I know you and Brody are getting pretty close."

Number two on her list of subjects she hoped wouldn't be mentioned. Jess didn't want to say anything she shouldn't, so she just didn't say anything at all.

"Jess, I really like Brody. And he's a hell of a ball player—one of the best I've seen. But I'm concerned about a lot of things." He took in a few deep breaths as though he were trying to inhale a bunch of letters that would rearrange themselves in his head and form the right words for him to exhale. "He's going off to college at the end of this year, and you still have another year of high school."

"Yeah." She didn't like that, either.

He leaned forward in his chair and placed his elbows on his knees. "I'm concerned about a long-distance relationship."

"Dad, we'll be okay. We've already discussed it."

"I know you *think* you'll be okay. It's one thing to discuss it. It's another thing to live it. It's not easy."

Jess knew it was best not to argue. "Okay, Dad."

"Now, I know you know I caught the two of you kissing yesterday."

She blushed and looked away.

His posture changed drastically and he wrung his hands together. "Jess, I know you're at an age now where your body is changing and you have certain … urges."

Jess's eyes opened wide and she couldn't help it when the laughter inside her burst forth. "Dad, are you trying to talk to me about sex?"

His embarrassment was evident. "Too late?" He raised an eyebrow.

"Too late as in do I know about sex, or too late as in have I had sex?"

"Both. Or neither. Hell, I don't know, Jess." He rubbed the sweat off his palms and onto his jeans. "Ever since your mom left … what do sixteen-year-old girls do?"

"Well, this one hasn't had sex yet," she said softly and her dad's shoulders sagged with relief.

"Thank God!" he gushed and flopped back into his chair. "You just made this old man gain a few years back on his life."

Jess giggled.

Her dad sat up and looked at her. "So, you're not going to be late for school again and you're not having sex with Brody," he said, presumably more for his own confirmation than asking for a response.

"Right," Jess answered anyway.

"Good. Now I have one more thing to talk about, and then you can go."

Third thing on her list, she thought glumly.

"I got a call from your boss today, and he said you might have the opportunity to take a trip to Montego Bay."

"Yeah." Damn that George.

"Okay."

Jess thought she must have misheard him. "Okay, what?"

"Okay, you can go."

"Just like that?" She wasn't hoping for a fight about it. She was just expecting one.

"Yes. Just like that. You're going to take your schoolwork with you, though."

"I am?"

"You're growing up, J-Bird, as much as I hate to admit it." He ran his fingers through his thinning hair. "At some point in life I have to hope that I've done my job and trust that you know what you're doing when you're not around me. I don't want to hold you back anymore. I don't want to be so overprotective that you miss out on life."

Jess jumped off the couch and threw her arms around his neck. "Thank you, Daddy! Thank you so much!"

"You're welcome." He grinned bashfully. Jess sat back down. Even though he'd said that was the last item on his list for discussion, she felt there was still more conversation to come. And she was correct. "Stay right there." He stood, a boyish grin replacing the tension on his face. "I have something for you."

Jess's mind was in a daze for the umpteenth time that day. She could still keep her job. She could still be with Brody and, she assumed, it was even okay to kiss him in front of her dad. And she was going to Jamaica. But she still had a fourth item on her list he hadn't mentioned yet, and if he came back into the room with her mom on his arm, she was going to be *very* disappointed.

Thankfully, though, he entered the room carrying a large black duffel bag adorned with a big white bow and set it down in front of her. "I don't know if it's something you wanted or if you can even use it, but I think I got a great deal, anyway." He sat back down in his chair to watch her open her gift. Jess couldn't help but take in how happy her dad looked at that moment. Younger. Less troubled.

She couldn't imagine what dwelled inside the bag at her feet, but she didn't waste much time. She greedily pulled the zipper and peered in. When she saw the camera she almost lost control of her bodily functions. "No freaking way," she said in disbelief. She began to pull everything out of the bag – cables and lenses and memory cards and instruction manuals for everything. "No freaking *way*!"

He looked amused. "Is that a good 'no freaking way'?"

"Dad, this is a Nikon D3X."

"Is that good?"

"Is that *good*?" she echoed. How could he not know? How could someone *not* know what a Nikon D3X was? Good? No. This was *way* beyond good. "How did you get this?"

He looked down sheepishly. "I bought it at a yard sale for a hundred bucks."

Jess blinked animatedly. "A hundred bucks?" She was about to burst. "Dad, this is an eight-thousand dollar camera."

He whistled low.

"Plus there are four other lenses in here—zoom, telephoto, wide angle, a teleconverter—there's more in this bag than I know what to do with. Dad, this camera is better than George's camera."

"So I did well then?"

She once again wrapped her arms around her father in complete and utter joy and disbelief. "You hit the lottery."

****

Brody's voice erupted as he picked up the phone halfway through the first ring. "Oh, thank God!"

Jess was instantly worried and she clutched the receiver in both hands. "What's wrong?"

"You said you'd call me at 6:00 and it's 6:45."

She relaxed a little, knowing Brody's dad was authoritarian when it came to his schedule: up at 5:30, shower at 6:00, breakfast at 6:45. He was only allowed to use the phone in the evening between 6:00 and 7:00, so they'd missed out on 45 minutes of conversation time. "I'm sorry. Dad decided to take me out for dinner and we just got back. Are you okay?"

"I'm . . . yeah. I'm okay."

Jess reevaluated the tone in Brody's voice. He didn't sound upset over their shortened conversation. He sounded more upset over the possibilities as to why she was late. He was never overprotective, and occasionally chastised her father for being so. And he didn't have a jealous side that she had ever seen. She didn't know what he was thinking or what to say to make it right.

Brody answered her question when he broke the silence between them. "I … thought your dad was going to keep you from me."

Once again she was still. Once again she was overwhelmed.

"Jess?"

"I'm here," she whispered.

"Did you get into trouble?"

"Surprisingly, no." Jess began to recap the earlier conversation she'd had with her dad.

"So, he didn't see where my hand was, then?" He was back to his usual playful manner.

Jess laughed to herself. Though he hadn't been touching anything he shouldn't have, his hand had been under her shirt, skin against skin on the small of her back. "He didn't mention it." Jess faintly heard Brody's dad in the background announcing it was 6:58.

"You don't have to work tomorrow, right?" he asked.

"No. Not until Friday."

"I'll pick you up for school then?"

"Sounds good."

"You going to my game?" He sounded hopeful.

She thought about teasing him and telling him no, but she knew he had less than two minutes on the phone. "I'll be there," she answered instead.

Brody's dad picked up another line. "Homework, Brody."

"Yes, sir," he said glumly.

"Tell Jessica good night." The line clicked when he hung up the phone.

Jess couldn't suppress her quick burst of anger. "Does he have a stopwatch in his ass?"

"No," Brody chuckled. "But I've thought about ramming one up there a time or two."

She giggled. "I'll see you in the morning."

"I'll see you in my dreams."

"Those better not be X-rated dreams," Jess said through her smile.

"I'll never tell."

Chapter Three

Even at the tender age of eight, Jess knew there was more vodka in her mother's glass than water. "Rotten kid," she slurred, flopping clumsily into her chair and sloshing her drink over the rim. She lit a cigarette and pulled in hard with her first drag. "You're so much like your father." She exhaled a plume of smoke.

Jess wiped at the steady flow of tears with the back of one hand as she absentmindedly twirled her hair with the other. Her cheek still stung from where she'd been struck.

"Well? What are you waiting for?" She hissed through nicotine-stained teeth. "Clean it up!"

Jess looked at the small pool of milk on the table. Hardly more than an ounce. Hardly worth a hard slap across the face. She stood stiffly and walked toward the kitchen to get a towel.

"And quit playing with your hair or I'll shave you bald."

Jess's eyes opened and her hands went straight to her head to make sure her mother hadn't made good on her threat once again. Remembering that she was no longer a young child and her mother had split without a trace more than seven years ago, she heaved a sigh and got ready for school.

Her dad seemed to sense some anxiety in his only child as she solemnly ate breakfast. "You okay, J-Bird?" She looked up from her cereal and his eyes darted to her left hand, which was entangled in the hair at her temple. "Oh." He looked away.

Jess realized what she was doing and quickly stopped. Her dad and Brody both knew of the nervous habit she had often as a small child, but recently only when she reminisced about her mother.

She felt a little better a half hour later when the doorbell announced the arrival of her boyfriend, but he too seemed to sense something amiss. He too instinctively looked at her left side for any hair out of place. He didn't turn from it as her father had, however. Jess looked into his eyes as he looked into hers. "Another bad dream?"

"You already know the answer to that, don't you?" She smiled feebly.

"She can't hurt you anymore, Jess." He slowly tucked the tangled hair behind her ear, and in the same movement, tilted her face up to his with his palm and kissed her gently. Jess parted her lips slightly to let him know she wanted more, and he didn't disappoint. His hand plunged deeper into her hair, his free arm snaking around her waist and pulling her into him.

Every thought of her dream forgotten, Jess returned Brody's kiss fervently, taking the collar of his sweatshirt in both hands. She was aware of every breath he took, every breath she took. She smelled the soap on his face, felt the warmth of his hands where he touched her, and then became amused when she felt stubble on his chin he had missed when he'd shaved that morning.

Brody pulled back. "Why are you smiling?"

Jess rubbed the rough spot on his jaw. "In a hurry?"

"Yes." He blushed. "I knew I was going to get to see my girlfriend before school and I was so excited I rushed out the door with a half-assed shave."

"Wow. Your girlfriend must be pretty special."

Brody's grin widened. "Well, she's not 'lick the windows on the short bus' special. But she's special nonetheless."

Jess's mouth was agape in mocked offense and she playfully socked Brody in the arm. "That wasn't very nice."

"C'mon. Let's go." He took her by the hand and started to lead her to the door.

"Oh, wait! I completely forgot to show you what my dad bought for me yesterday!" Jess proceeded to show the contents of the black duffel bag to Brody. "I can't wait to show George tomorrow, and I'm going to take some pictures at your game today. To try it out a little."

He put his hand firmly on her waist. "Well, if I'm late for school they won't let me play. We have to go." Brody ushered her out the door.

"You're the best player on the team," Jess argued, letting him lead her down the walk anyway. "You could sleep with the coach's wife and he'd still let you play."

Brody blushed for the second time that morning. "I don't know if I'd go *that* far."

****

Game days were tense for Brody. He always felt he should be allowed to skip class and go straight to the field to reflect and focus from his place behind the dish. He was there mentally all day, anyway. In English his mind wasn't on proper sentence structure and grammar. It was on proper field etiquette and conduct. In Chemistry, his mind began on the periodic table of elements and wandered to the defensive hand signals Coach Traynor had given him the day before. And in his lame, easy-A pottery class he wasn't worried about the timing on the kiln to keep his ashtray from shattering. He was worried about the timing on his throw to second to keep the runner from stealing.

Jess's mood had seemed to lighten as the day wore on, but Brody's only became more intense. He thought for sure that the school day would never end, and was already at the door with his hand on the knob when the final bell rang. Not even bothering to put his backpack away, he headed straight for the locker room to suit up. The first one to the field, he dropped his gear off in the dugout and looked for Jess in her usual place right behind home plate. Right behind *him*.

"Smile." She snapped his picture, looked at the image on the screen, and wolf whistled. "Damn. I don't know who the hell this guy is, but he's pretty hot."

Brody blew a kiss at Jess and turned back around. This was his place. He breathed in the freshly cut grass in the outfield, the damp dirt in the infield, the hot dogs and popcorn in the concession stands. He felt the heat of the sun on his face combined with the bite of a chilly late-winter breeze. He heard his teammates slowly making their way to the dugout and the fans filling the bleachers. This was where he belonged.

He turned once more to Jess, returned her smile, and joined his team.

Both games flew by for Brody, and Spanish Springs turned out to be a formidable opponent. He did as his teammates had predicted and hit three home runs: one in the first game, two in the second. Each time he knew he'd hit solid. Each time he watched the ball hit the bat on the sweet spot. Each time he sensed it would go over the fence, just by the deep pinging noise it made when white cowhide connected with blue aluminum.

He left the field satisfied. Exhilarated. Victorious. Exhausted.

He showered quickly knowing that Jess would be waiting for him.

"My hero," she said huskily as he stepped outside.

Brody shook his head dog-like, splattering her with water from his freshly washed hair. "How do you like me now?"

Jess wiped her chin with the palm of her hand and grinned. "Well, I've always thought you were kind of an asshole." She answered with her half-smile. "Now I realize you're a whole ass."

He bent over and kissed her cheek. "Took you long enough." Brody picked up his bag and hers in one hand, draped his other arm casually over her shoulder, and led her toward the parking lot.

"Where are we going?"

"Made a deal with my dad," Brody said. "One hour with you for every home run I hit tonight."

She stopped walking. "I get you for three whole hours?"

Brody couldn't believe he had agreed to it, either. His dad wasn't mean, but he was very militant. Most dads wanted their sons to be the next best athlete with the multi-million dollar contract. Most dads never got to watch their sons achieve that. Brody's dad, knowing that his son had the talent, wanted to make sure he didn't do anything to blow his chances. He was dictatorial over every aspect of his life. He had even tried to get him to stop seeing Jess, but Brody had made sure to let him know that wasn't going to happen. "If you make me break up with Jess, I've played my last game of baseball," he had said. His dad apparently had believed him. He agreed they could still date, but he did limit his time with her.

"Three whole hours," Brody echoed as they started walking again. "Would have been four, but that right fielder made a hell of a catch."

"I know. I got a picture of it."

Now it was Brody's turn to stop his saunter. "You're kidding me." He sighed.

"What?" Jess seemed bewildered.

"We get to be together and do whatever we want for three whole hours, and you're going to show me pictures, aren't you?" He wasn't upset, really, because he did support Jess with her photography. He was just a little disappointed.

Jess smiled hugely. "Only for two hours and fifty-five minutes. The rest of the time we'll do what you want."

They reached Brody's car and he opened the trunk. "Your house or mine?"

"Depends on whether we want to deal with the Fornication Officer or the Clock Nazi."

Brody laughed out loud. "Well, first things first," he said. "I'm starving to death."

****

It never ceased to amaze Jess just how much Brody could eat. They decided to raid a fast-food drive-thru and take everything back to the now deserted ball field dugout, which would have been romantic, except it smelled like feet. She watched as he downed his sixth cheeseburger and didn't realize she was smirking until he said, "What?" with his cheeks still puffed with food.

"Nothing," she snickered. "You're just so cute."

"Cute?" He swallowed half a cheeseburger in one gulp. "I was going for ruggedly handsome."

"Well, with your mouth full and mustard on your chin, you get cute."

Brody set his soda down on the bench beside him and smiled as he wiped his chin with the back of his hand. "How about now?"

"That's more like it."

Her heart sped up as he leaned toward her and whispered in her ear. "How much time do I have left?"

Jess found it difficult to speak. "You passed your five minutes a long time ago."

Brody dropped to his knees in front of Jess and pressed her gently against the back of the concrete dugout. "Can I have five more?" He didn't wait for her answer. His lips tasted of cheeseburger with mustard, but Jess didn't care. She wondered if hers still carried a tang of her chicken sandwich, but Brody didn't seem too bothered with that, either.

Jess was vaguely aware of her surroundings: the sounds, the smells. She knew the train was passing, and she knew it should have been loud, but she barely heard it over the ringing in her ears and the thud of her own heartbeat. She no longer noticed the sunflower seed and teenage boy smell of the dugout. It was replaced by the faint scent of the shampoo in Brody's hair, the cologne he wore when they went out on dates, and fast food grease. She hardly realized that she was no longer vertical against the back of the dugout, but horizontal on the bench, his mouth still on hers. And she would have gone on that way for hours had Brody's right hand not found its way to her left breast.

"Brody, what the …" She sat up quickly.

"Oh, geez, Jess. I'm sorry." He sat, rejected and disappointed, on the hard concrete floor, his arms wrapped around his knees.

Jess took a moment to collect herself and ponder what had just happened. He had never done that before, and it took her by surprise. It wasn't that she didn't love him. In fact, she was pretty sure she could be with him forever. So what was the big deal?

She looked down at Brody, who was still apparently mentally abusing himself over what he'd done. He was just so adorable. She climbed down off the bench and onto the dugout floor. Taking Brody by the chin, she made him look into her eyes. The pained look on his face melted into a faint smile.

Jess kissed him on the end of his nose. "My turn. Let's go look at pictures now."

Brody nodded and stood, then offered his hand to Jess to help her up. When she was vertical again, she hugged him tightly around his middle. He seemed hesitant to return her embrace, and only lightly pressed his hands against her back.

"It's okay, Brody." She knew enough about him to know that he would continue to brood for a while, but then he would be okay.

He nodded again, and they headed for his car.

****

Stupid, stupid, stupid, stupid, Brody thought to himself as he drove. *Why the hell did I do that?* Well, he knew *why* he'd done it. He wanted to do it. He wanted to go further. But he knew better.

His mind replayed the moment over and over: her breath against his neck, warm and rapid, one hand on his lower back, one hand on his shoulder. His hand was on her waist, and he had moved it up a little, to test the waters. She didn't complain, and kissed him again. Optimistic, he slid his hand higher—on her ribcage now. He could feel her heartbeat pounding rapidly beneath his palm. A little higher, and still no protest from Jess. He had thought maybe this was it. Maybe this time. One more upward movement and he had reached his target.

Stupid, stupid, stupid.

His torment must have been obvious to Jess as he pulled into her driveway. "Do you still want to come in and look at pictures?"

"Of course I do." His time with her was valuable, and as long as they would be looking at pictures and not touching each other, he felt he could probably control his wandering hands. "I still have an hour and a half before I have to go home."

"Okay. You just seem … upset."

"I am a little. With myself," he admitted. "I'm sorry, Jess. Really. I was stupid." *Stupid, stupid, stupid.* "I hope I didn't ruin the rest of the night."

"Okay, now you *are* being stupid." She smiled and squeezed his leg just above his knee, giving him tingles that only reiterated his indiscretion. "Come on. Let's go."

Brody grabbed Jess's camera out of the trunk and walked with her hand-in-hand through the living room and to the computer in the den. They sat at the desk, but Brody immediately bounced back up to greet Jess's dad as he entered the room. "Mr. Waterford." He nodded and put out his hand.

Wesley shook the hand that was offered and returned the nod. "Nice work on that ball field today, son."

"Thank you, sir." Brody still didn't know how to act around Jess's father. It was different when the two of them were younger and they would play baseball together. But since they had begun to date, he'd always felt he was being looked at differently. Scrutinized. He had never asked Jess about it, but he was pretty sure he was right. And he couldn't really blame her dad, either. Especially after what he'd recently just done in the dugout … with the same hand he'd just used to shake Jess's father's. He looked at his palm to see if it looked any different now that it had groped Jess, and then quickly wiped the distastefulness off on his jeans.

"You get some good pictures tonight, Princess?"

"Yes, Daddy."

"So, that camera's working out for you?"

"So far, so good."

"Okay." Mr. Waterford cleared his throat. "Well, I'll leave you two alone, then."

Brody couldn't help but think Jess's dad was stalling to prevent their solitude even if they were only going to be one room away, and apparently Jess had the same idea.

"Bye, Daddy."

He stopped at the door. "Holler if you need anything."

"Dad!"

"I'm going. I'm going." He put his hands over his head in surrender and walked out of the room.

Brody sat back down next to Jess at the computer and she began to tick off picture after picture on the camera. His initial discomfort over his previous misconduct ceased a bit as he saw what was on the screen. The photos were amazing. Every one of them. Centered, focused, beautiful. Jess knew what she was doing, and each one was crystal clear, and completely perfect. "Wow."

She grinned from ear to ear. "Okay, now watch this." She plugged the camera into her computer and the images appeared on the larger monitor. They were even more vibrant and lucid than before.

"Jess," Brody was impressed. "These pictures are just great." He didn't really know what words to use to express how proud he was of her—how much he admired her talent.

"This one is my favorite." She clicked to a picture of Brody, his shin guards and chest pad on, his mask up on top of his helmet, his right arm fending off the third baseman who would steal his prize, the deep concentration on his face as he waited for the foul ball to come down into his mitt. She'd snapped the picture just as the ball was two feet from becoming an out. "I'm going to print this one."

A few clicks of the mouse and her printer churned in response. It was an older model, so it gurgled and spewed and coughed, and eventually ejected the finished product. Jess grabbed it from the tray before Brody had a chance to look.

"Well," she said in disgust. "What the hell is *that*?"

KIM HARNES

Chapter Four

"What the hell is what?" Jess barely heard Brody's voice as she stared at the repugnant flaw on the photo.

"This!" She stuffed the image in his face. "Look at the bottom left corner! There's a smudge!" She had noticed it instantly. It was an imperfection in her perfect photograph. And she was livid.

"I don't understand, Jess. It's a great picture."

"But look *here*." She pointed to the opaque block in the bottom left corner. "This isn't right." Jess was upset her Nikon D3X would betray her like that. No wonder her dad had gotten it so cheap. Where the photograph should have shown the left leg of the umpire, there was clearly something there that shouldn't have been. There was no reason it should have been flawed like that. "Damn camera." She didn't speak very loudly, but Brody heard it anyway.

"You can't blame the camera, Jess." He put his hand on her arm and she suddenly felt better. Consoled by his touch. "Maybe it's the computer. Or the printer."

He did have a point.

"I guess I can try to print it again."

"There ya go." Brody spoke placidly. "I'm sure it'll be fine."

A few more clicks of the mouse and the printer roiled to life a second time. It rocked to the left and swayed to the right again and again and again until it spit out the photo.

And it was exquisite.

Jess exhaled in a gush.

"See?" Brody said. "Perfect."

Jess looked into Brody's eyes and whispered softly, "Just like you." She slithered her hands up until they were lying flat on his chest.

But Brody took both her hands in his and held her at arm's length. "I'm far from perfect," he said solemnly. "And I should go."

Jess figured he was still agonizing over his imprudence, but she didn't want him to leave. "You still have a half hour," she protested.

"I know." He squeezed her hands in his. "But I have to include travel time and all that. And it's a school night, so …"

Jess deflated. Travel time was all of about five minutes. "Brody, what's wrong?"

"Walk me to my car?"

She realized she wasn't going to change his mind, and reluctantly followed him out the door.

****

Brody ended up spending his last half hour trying to explain to Jess why he had to leave a half hour early. She was very good at getting her way. But she had made him feel better. It was short-lived, however, and his dad met him at the door, looked at his watch, and shook his head disapprovingly.

"You're almost late," he grumbled.

"Doesn't that mean I'm on time?" Brody said under his breath and headed upstairs to his room. He flopped onto his bed.

He laid there for awhile—staring into the darkness, still fully dressed, flat on his back, his fingers laced behind his head, his feet crossed at the ankles, his smile unfaltering. He replayed the night over in his mind.

It would have been the perfect night with one notable boob-grabbing exception. The odious hand twitched involuntarily beneath him at the recollection.

It was easier to let it go this time, though, and his thoughts quickly turned to his plans for Friday and the upcoming weekend. Jess had to work in the morning, but since they'd played a doubleheader on a Thursday, he didn't have practice again until Monday after school. And all of that meant he could spend every waking moment from Friday afternoon until lights out Sunday with Jess. Well, every waking moment with the exception of his usual Saturday morning date with his dad where they went over the fundamentals of baseball. As if he hadn't had them drilled into his head enough. Brody was pretty confident that, with everything he'd been taught on and off the field, he could play his position exceptionally, and any position passably.

His dad had been a pitcher, though he was never good enough to be drafted out of college. He had wanted Brody to be a pitcher. Pitchers were the leaders of the team. Pitchers got the credit when the game went well. Pitchers, he had said, were the moneymakers.

And he had learned how to pitch to placate his dad.

But Brody had always wanted to catch. He wanted to lead the team from behind the plate and not from upon the mound. He wanted to dictate the pitches that were thrown instead of throwing what was dictated. He wanted to … well … play the whole game.

It was funny to Brody how his mind always wandered to one of two things—baseball, and Jess. He made sure to redirect his attention to the latter as he drifted off to sleep.

****

Jess yawned. Her dad was fairly lenient about her bedtime, and she was still awake choosing the pictures that would gain permanence onto glossy paper.

The printer stirred loudly on the desk as it recreated Jess's photographic brilliance. She waited as the last chug died before she picked up the stack sitting idly in the tray.

The left fielder making a catch.

Jason Boggs throwing a knuckle ball.

The second baseman stepping on the bag and throwing to first to complete the double play.

"It's getting late, J-Bird." Her dad peeked his head into the room and pulled her back to reality. "You have work tomorrow. Are you going to bed soon?"

"Yeah, Dad." Jess yawned again. "Just finishing up these last pictures. Some of them are pretty good." She handed the stack over.

He looked at each, filing the one he'd examined behind the ones he hadn't. "These are great." It wasn't a fatherly "great," but an admiring "great."

Jess smiled in appreciation.

"What's this here, though?" He showed a photo to Jess she hadn't looked at yet.

"What's what?" She quickly took the picture from her father's grasp and inspected it. It didn't take a half second before she noticed its defect in the top right corner. "Damn it."

"Pardon?" her dad mused, an eyebrow raised.

"Sorry, Dad. It's just … this is the second picture that's been smudged." She tried to rub the unpleasantness off the photograph, but was unsuccessful. "I'm just a little disappointed. I'm hoping it's not the camera."

Jess watched as her dad's shoulders slumped.

"I mean … I'm sure it's not the camera," she stammered. "It's probably just the older printer or the computer."

Jess's intentions were good, but her mention of the older printer and computer only seemed to add to his discomfort. She knew he had tried to supply the best of everything for her, but, being a one-income family, he'd had his struggles.

"Dad, I … I didn't mean … everything is great," she said finally.

"No. It's not great. But it's what you have for now."

"But …"

"Jess, it's okay. I know you get it. And you appreciate what you have. And you know I'd give more if I could." Her father looked at the remaining pictures in his hands. "And I know you're going to make so much more of yourself than I ever did."

Jess stood and hugged him. "If I do, Dad," she said as she squeezed his middle, "it's because you made it happen."

Her father returned the hug. "You have so much talent."

Jess felt a single drop fall down her cheek. "I love you, Dad."

"Yeah," he teased and wiped his own tear with the back of his hand. "I know."

Jess sniffled and laughed at the same time. "A bit confident, huh?"

"A little bit." He looked at her intently. "I'm so proud of you, Jess."

"After what you've been through, Dad," Jess said, taking his upper arms in her hands, "I'm so proud of you, too. You rock."

Jess's father lowered his head and touched noses with his daughter. "You should think about going to bed. It's getting late."

Jess smiled and motioned to her pile of photographs still in her dad's hand. "Let me put the rest of this away, and I'll be upstairs in a few minutes."

He handed over the pictures. Jess caught him out of the corner of her eye as he watched her for a little while from the doorway. She meticulously and carefully put her camera and all of its components back into the black duffel bag, and Jess noticed he only turned away after she sat back down at the computer, the pile of pictures in her hands.

She rifled through them briefly, opened the top drawer of the desk, and deposited both of the flawed photos atop a thin layer of discarded bills and receipts. She looked at them in disgust once again, set the unmarred pictures by the monitor, and then slammed the offensive drawer closed and headed off to bed.

Chapter Five

"You ruined my life. You know that, right?"
Amanda Waterford snuffed out her cigarette into an
already overflowing ashtray.

Jess just sat there. Unmoving. She'd heard all this
before.

"You ruined my body. My career. If I hadn't had
you, I'd still be modeling right now."

Jess fought back the tears that threatened to
escape. She poked at her cereal with her spoon, watching
the multi-colored sugary puffs sink on her command, and
then bob back to the surface on their own volition.

"Miserable little devil child," she hissed. She
slapped a new pack of cigarettes against her palm
several times, viciously ripped off the cellophane
wrapper, pulled out a fresh Camel, and set the end
aflame with her bright orange lighter.

Jess continued to absentmindedly prod at her
breakfast with the spoon in her right hand as she twisted
her hair with her left, and was snapped back into reality
by a hard blow to the right side of her head.

"Stop that!"

Jess, in her surprise over being hit, sent her right
hand straight down into her cereal bowl spilling most of
its contents onto the vinyl tablecloth. Her left hand
gripped tighter. Tight enough that the pain in her left
temple from pulling her hair was worse than her right
where she'd been belted by her mother's closed fist.

The tears came for Jess then. "I'm sorry,
Mommy!" she wailed, instantly jumping up from the table
and getting a towel to clean the mess. "I was so clumsy.
I'm sorry." Jess began to frantically sop up the milk with
the towel, anticipating her mother's next move. Waiting

for the next wallop. Not knowing where it was coming or when.

She didn't have to wait long.

She heard the thud before she felt it in her side as her mother brought her foot into her ribcage and sent Jess sprawling across the table face first into her own spilled breakfast. Her bottom teeth pierced her lip as her chin hit the table and the air in her lungs left in a whoosh. She gasped frantically as she fought against her own body's refusal to breathe.

She lie there, spread out on the table, her eyes wide with fear, and watched her mother continue to casually smoke her cigarette as she wheezed painfully for what she thought was her last breath. The embers on the end burned hot as her mother inhaled its toxicity.

Amanda only showed concern when it suited her needs, and that need presented itself when Jess's dad entered the kitchen. "What happened?" His cheeks were flushed, his shirt half-buttoned, his tool belt gripped tightly in his hand.

"She slipped," Amanda said quickly and took another long drag off her cigarette. "She slipped on something on the floor and fell into the table." She exhaled a cloud of smoke.

"Jess?" She felt her dad's warm hands on her waist, but her side screamed with pain. "Are you okay?"

Jess slumped onto the floor, coughed once, and spit red.

"What happened here?" he demanded.

"What, Wesley?" Amanda spat. "What do you think happened? She fell. Just like I said."

Wesley picked up his daughter as she looked up at him with her tear-streaked face. He gingerly loaded her into the car, and drove her to the hospital.

Three bruised ribs and four stitches in her lip that time. But she fell. That's what the doctors heard, anyway. She's such an awkward and clumsy seven-year-old girl, Amanda protested. She slipped and fell into the table. Only the two of them knew she really slipped and fell into a size seven Nike.

When Jess's eyes opened, her bedroom walls looked bright white and she shook her head and blinked until they faded to the normal pale green. Her side ached out of recollection, and she could sense the salty metallic taste of blood in her mouth. She hurried to the bathroom to brush her teeth.

****

"Again?" Brody smoothed the hair at Jess's left temple and pulled her solidly into his chest, wrapping his arms around her as her body trembled against him.

"George made me go lie down in the lounge." Her voice was muffled against his shoulder. "I didn't even get to show him my camera."

"Jess, Baby, maybe you should go home."

"No!"

Her abrupt defiance made him release her quickly, as though she would suddenly spontaneously combust.

"Sorry," she said quietly and nestled back into him. Brody reciprocated, though a little more cautiously. "But if I go home on a Friday, my dad will keep me home all weekend. Not to mention the fact that I'll have to explain to him what's wrong. And I'll get over this. It was just … bad this time. They've been getting more and more vivid—the memories, I mean."

The bell rang causing Jess to jump in Brody's arms and he held her tighter despite the fact that he knew he needed to let her loose. He only released her when he determined holding her for one second longer would make them both late for class. He didn't care for himself, really. He'd just captained the winning team in a double-header the day before and his homeroom teacher was a baseball fan. But he couldn't let Jess get into trouble. Not after the morning she'd had. He took her hand and began to walk her to her class, which was more than half the distance of the school away from his own.

"What are you doing? You'll be late."

"Oh, Mr. Murdock won't care. He was at the game, remember?" Brody smirked. "Besides, even if he does care, you're more important to me right now than a tardy slip."

Jess's mood seemed to brighten a bit. "Only right now?"

"Yeah. Just this morning," he countered.

"Jerkwad."

They arrived at her classroom door and Brody straightened the hair at her left temple again causing Jess to blush. "She's not worth it." He kissed her cheek. "Don't think about what she did in your past. Think about what you want to do with me this weekend."

She smiled and lowered her voice sexily. "Oh, the things I want to do with you this weekend."

Tingles spread throughout his body. "Tease." He kissed her hand as he released it and strode toward his own classroom.

****

"Take my picture, Jess!" her dad shouted joyfully.

*"Nuh uh," Jess waddled around the coffee table
and away from her dad's outstretched arms, giggling all
the way, her diaper sagging almost to mid-thigh, the
white plastic Fisher Price camera in her clutches. The
usual curtain of smoke clung to her mother like a gray-
black aura. "Mommy's da model. I take her picture. Boys
can't be models." She raised the camera and pressed the
button several times, advancing the cubed flash a quarter
turn counter clockwise with each click.*

*"Get that thing away from me." Her mother
pushed the toy into Jess's face causing her to cry loudly.*

*"Oh, come on, Amanda. She was just playing."
Wesley dropped to his knees by Jess to tend to her bloody
nose.*

*She snatched the toy from Jess's hand and threw
it against the wall, the larger piece dropping to the floor,
the multi-colored faux flashbulb soaring across the room
and landing behind the Christmas tree. "Do I look like
I'm in the mood to play?" she scoffed.*

"Jessica?"

Jess snapped her head toward the mention of her
full name. It took a few seconds for her thoughts to
completely surface from the depths of her daydream.
"Yes, Miss Price?"

"Jessica, your nose is bleeding. Do you need to
see the nurse?"

She took the tissue her teacher offered and dabbed
at the moisture surrounding her left nostril. To her
surprise, a dark crimson stain appeared. "No, thank you.
This will be fine."

When the bell rang, Jess gathered her books and
trekked back to her locker. The flow of blood had
stopped, but her curiosity hadn't. She couldn't imagine
what had caused her nosebleed. It certainly couldn't have

been merely the memory of being thumped in the face with a hard plastic toy. Could it? Well, no, of course it couldn't. That was Heinz 57 different varieties of ridiculous.

Maybe she reacted to the daydream and accidentally hit herself in the nose. That, at least, made a little more sense.

She gingerly pressed her thumb and index finger against the bridge of her nose. Surely she would know if she'd hit herself if she squeezed—ever so slightly.

No pain.

Strange.

"You seemed vexed, my vixen." Brody sidled up to her when she reached her locker.

Jess forgot about her dismay for a moment and grinned her half grin"What the hell—?" Brody's face changed and concern replaced casual.

"What?"

"You have blood on your face."

"Oh, that." Jess wiped at her lip with the soiled tissue that was still in her hand. "My nose started to bleed in English. It stopped, though."

Brody's concern vanished and he smirked deucedly. "I thought I'd warned you about picking your nose in class."

Jess's heart lightened. "I couldn't help myself. I saved the booger for you, though."

"No, you keep it this time." Brody pressed his lips to Jess's ear. "But if you feel the urge to dig for gold again, at least cut your fingernails." He kissed her neck and strolled to his next class.

As the chills from her encounter with Brody wore off, her thoughts reverted back to her lousy morning. First she'd dreamt about her mother. Then George had forced her to lie down instead of work ("You don't look right, Jess," he had said to her dismay, deep lines creasing his aged brow. He didn't seem to notice the extra slump that appended her already defeated posture at his dismissal. "Maybe you should just go to the lounge and relax today. I can handle it."). Then a twenty-minute bus ride she usually enjoyed, but today was barely conscious for, followed by yet another memory of her mother about a bloody nose, which somehow resulted in a real bloody nose.

And she also stewed over Brody's incessant desire to cheer her up.

It wasn't that she minded his comfort so much, but she still felt badly that he thought he needed to. She didn't like to be the weak, dependent girlfriend. She liked to be the strong, confident one. She liked to have Brody console her, but she despised it when she needed consoling.

She sometimes wondered what it would have been like to have a mother to talk to. A real mother. One that was caring and loving that would listen and give advice. One that wasn't crass and vulgar and harsh and abrupt. One that wasn't in-your-face honest and kick-your-ass violent.

Because she didn't have that.

Ever.

And what she did have was gone. She had run off to find the greener grass on the other side. And she had apparently found it, because she never came back.

KIM HARNES

Chapter Six

As usual, Brody's eyes opened before his alarm sounded. The last remnants of his dream still spun in his mind and settled on the face of his mother. He wondered if he'd dreamed of her because of Jess's overwhelming recollection of her own mother, or if there were some other trigger.

Brody's mother had died right around the same time Jess's had left home. This had strengthened their friendship immensely, as they had leaned upon each other for comfort and support.

But Amanda Waterford and Samantha Campbell were two completely different beings. Where Jess's mom was an abusive alcoholic, Brody's mom was doting and affectionate. A stay-at-home mom that cooked and cleaned and made bacon and eggs and pancakes for breakfast, who packed healthy sack lunches, a snack after school, and then cooked a dinner fit for a king. His socks and jeans were always without holes and grass stains, and his baseball uniform was the whitest on the field. When his team won the game, she was sure to have a special treat for everyone, and she was there to give a hug when they lost.

And she was so good to Jess.

In fact, the dream he had just awakened from was of the day Brody had first introduced Jess to his mom. The day of their first baseball game.

"Mom, this is my friend Jess," Brody had said, *motioning to the scrawny girl to his right that was hopping gingerly from one foot to the other.*

"Well, hello, Jess." Brody's mom had seemed a *bit distraught over her haggard appearance: the holes in*

her hand-me-down uniform, the tangles in her hair ... the bruise on her cheek.

Jess had then spit into her hand and offered it to Brody's mother, her usual blob of gum taking up half the space in her mouth.

"So nice to meet you," she said sweetly, spit into her own hand with all the femininity she could muster for an act of that nature, and shook Jess's with reciprocal vigor.

"Okay, so I gotta go pee before the game, so I'll catch ya later." Jess had hiked up her pants, adjusted her cap, turned, and scuttled off.

Brody's mom had grinned. "Catch ya later," she called after her, and she watched as Jess ran toward the port-a-potties, one hand on her hat to keep it on her head, the other hand between her legs as if to hold it all in. Jess paused at the outhouse and stared blankly as if wondering which part she could afford to let go of so she could open the door, opted for the one on her head, tugged hard, and scurried inside, not even waiting for the door to hinge shut before she yanked down her pants and sat down. Brody's mom turned to him and ruffled his hair. "I like her," she said. "But she's so skinny."

And every day after that, Brody had found an extra sandwich in his lunchbox.

The sweet memory of his mother faded in loathsome anticipation of Baseball 101 with his father. He dressed slowly, retrieved his mitt from his dresser, and meandered to the back yard, the chill of the morning biting his cheeks the instant he opened the door. His dad was already there, a bat in one hand, a baseball in the other, gnashing his teeth as he eyed his watch. "Let's go." He took a swing at the ball.

STILL PHOTO

****

Brody called at 11:00. "How are you feeling?"

Jess lay back on her bed. She was dressed, but lounging, waiting for him to pick her up. "Better."

"Good."

Jess sensed relief in his voice. "I had a better dream last night. About your mom this time instead of mine."

"What was it about?"

"The day I met her at our baseball game when I had to pee so bad."

Brody chuckled. "How weird is it that I had the same dream?"

"You did not!"

"I really did."

"That *is* weird."

"So, where am I taking you today?"

Jess had been planning all morning, so she was ready with her answer. "We're hiking up Peavine."

"That's a long walk," he said. "What are you going to do with me when we get to the top?"

"That's for me to know and you to find out," she said playfully.

"I'll be there in thirty seconds."

She laughed and headed downstairs. "But it takes you five minutes to get here."

"But I left my house four and a half minutes ago."

The doorbell rang. "And you sped." She ran to the door and flung it open.

"Nah. I just hit all the green lights."

Jess gasped. Brody stood there, his cell phone in his left hand at his side, a red rose in his right hand in front of him, his wrist still clad in the thin leather bracelet she had made him for Christmas seven years ago. The light northern breeze pressed his t-shirt against his left side revealing the taut muscles of his abdomen. The cotton rippled across his chest and the loose hem at his right side flapped lazily. His hat was on backward, and his sandy-blond hair stuck out boyishly from the clasp at his forehead. But what caught her most was his expression. Fervent and desirous, yet casual and charming, it was a look that said, "I want you, but I get it."

"Are you going to let me in, or am I going hiking with your garden gnome?" he quipped.

Jess felt the embarrassment spread across her face straining her cheeks and blazing them crimson. She opened the door wider, stepped backward to allow him entrance, and accepted the flower he offered. She pressed it to her nose to take in its fragrance and exhaled delightfully. Then she wrapped her free arm around Brody's neck and locked her lips to his. "Thank you," she said when they separated. "I love roses."

"I know you do." Brody followed her into the kitchen and sat on a bar stool as he watched her take a vase down from the cupboard, fill it with water, and gingerly engulf the stem in its depths.

"Are you ready to go?" she asked him.

He looked down at his feet. "I think we'll have to go back to my house to get my boots. I guess I jumped the gun leaving early, but I wanted to see you."

He looked away, apparently ashamed at his own eagerness.

Jess skulked along the kitchen counter, making sure Brody was watching as she lovingly caressed the rose he'd gifted her with and inhaled its scent once more. Then she demurely bit her bottom lip and sidled toward him, her fingers still tracing the last petal. She reached his extended arms and pressed herself against his chest as he slid the palms of his hands around her trim waist. She could feel his heartbeat quicken, matching the rapid pulse of her own. She breathed in the sweetness of him: the intoxicating mixture of soap and shampoo and toothpaste and deodorant and cologne and just a hint of mustard, which he ate on everything.

She could have stayed there forever.

"You smell so good." She exhaled against his neck and felt his body quiver. Encouraged, she pressed her lips against his skin. His hands still firm against the small of her back, he pulled her closer into him. Jess traced her fingertips up the firm muscles on either side of Brody's spine and her lips trailed slowly from the nape of his neck to the base of his ear and he let out a quick, soft moan.

He kissed her just above her collarbone, then, and tingles spread to her extremities. Finally unable to take it any longer, Jess took his face in her hands and their mouths met. Their breathing accelerated simultaneously, each of their arms wrapping tightly around the other.

Jess twisted her hips inward, felt something against her leg, and grinned malevolently.

"You are evil." He pushed her away gently and stood, the smirk still touching his eyes. "Let's go get my boots."

Jess, having obtained the reaction she desired, kissed his cheek, and took his hand in hers. "You have to get that in your car first." She motioned toward the large black duffel bag next to the front door and pulled her sweatshirt over her tank top as they left the house.

Brody's metallic blue '67 Chevy Impala had more than enough trunk space for Jess's bag, and he heaved it in with little effort. He secured the trunk and led her to the passenger side door, opened it chivalrously, and closed it behind her.

Jess checked her makeup in the side mirror as Brody walked around the front of the car, and almost screamed out loud when, instead of her own face, she saw the reflection of her mother—pallid and thin, her hollow cheeks only slightly less sunken than the deep-set and vacant gray eyes staring blankly back at her. But as quickly as she was there, she was gone again, and Jess shook the image from her mind as Brody slid into the driver's seat. "Are you okay?"

Jess attempted to quickly compose herself. "I'm … I'm fine."

"Okay, then I have just one question for you."

"What's that?"

He turned the key and revved the powerful engine. "Who's gonna lug that bag up the hill?"

Jess couldn't resist Brody's charm, and she felt her dimples crimp her cheeks. "The bestest boyfriend on the planet."

"Will he be joining us, then?"

****

The longer they slogged up the hill, the heavier the bag became, and the deeper the strap buried itself into Brody's shoulder. "What do you have in this thing, anyway?" He had a pretty good idea, of course. Her camera and all its components had to be in there, as he was fairly sure it was the zoom lens tunneling into his hip. But what he couldn't make out were the clanking metal noises and the sharp object that had been stabbing him in his posterior since he had last adjusted the bag.

"Stuff," she panted over her shoulder.

Brody had made sure Jess was in front of him as they hiked. He had told her it was so he'd be there to catch her if she fell backward, but his ulterior motive was to watch the ampleness within her tight jeans shift from side to side as she climbed the steep trail.

"Stuff," he grumbled, hitched the bag upward again, winced at the poke in his derrière, and trudged onward.

As they ascended the canyon the surroundings changed drastically. The droning of the freeway faded behind them, as well as the smell of sagebrush and wildflowers—thick and overpowering like a cloud of bad perfume. They were replaced by the crunching of their footsteps on the carpet of dehydrated pinion pine needles and the ancillary blessed scent of clean air and damp earth. Though he was athletic, the climb was mostly vertical, and the stitch in his side increased annoyingly due to the thinning air that accompanied the rise in altitude. He didn't fail to notice Jess's mutual fatigue.

"Do you need to take a break?" His attempt at valiancy was mostly so he could catch his own breath, and he hoped she hadn't noticed.

Jess apparently wasn't fooled. "Nah, I'm good." She stopped and turned. "You want me to take the bag for a little while?" she taunted.

Brody took the strap from his shoulder and lowered the increasingly heavy canvas sack to the ground and grinned. Jess's smirk vanished. "Come get it," he challenged.

"You're not serious."

"I'm not?" He wiped the sweat off his forehead with the back of his hand and replaced his hat, the hair once protruding from it now matted and sweaty.

Jess eyed him curiously, and Brody figured she was sizing him up and deciding upon whether he was really serious or not. He couldn't hold the smile back any longer, and he barely ducked in time to avoid the pine cone she had thrown at his head.

"You're a jackass, Jackass!" she bellowed.

"Good arm, Babe! I'm gonna warn Boggsie he's got competition!"

"You're just lucky I didn't have a bat!" she retorted and turned back toward the trail. "I'd have swung for the fence. Left temple, right on the sweet spot."

"Ooh. Such violence." Brody chuckled lightly, but then frowned when he was reminded of the offensive sack at his feet. Though the short break had eased some of the strain in his back, it didn't lighten the load any, and he hoped Jess hadn't heard him groan as he lifted the strap to his shoulder for the last leg of their journey. The familiar jab in his backside, though more than mildly irritating, only broadened his grin as he memorized the pattern on the decorative embroidered pockets of Jess's jeans.

Twenty minutes later, they reached a secluded pond amidst a forest of pines. Brody couldn't believe its splendor. The pond itself wasn't swimmable by any means, but it was crisp and calm, and the bright spring sun bounced off it and spilled its amber reflection onto Jess's pale, beautiful face. He took in a breath, but barely remembered to exhale until Jess's delicate voice brought him back to reality.

"We're here." She lifted her arms triumphantly and turned toward Brody. "We made it. Finally."

Brody lowered the bag, which he was sure now weighed more than his car, and set it atop a large granite boulder. He quickly forgot about the twinge in his shoulder, however, and wrapped both his arms around Jess's midsection. "So, your plan was to exhaust me so I couldn't make a pass?" he teased.

Jess laughed. "No, my plan was to build your appetite, and then feed you." She unzipped the bag and produced a blanket and a basket of food, and he peered in to confirm the presence of her camera, still not seeing the one item he was looking for.

"So, what's in there that was poking me in the butt?"

Jess looked confused. "There isn't anything pokey in there. The forks are in the basket."

Brody rifled through the remaining contents and only saw camera equipment. He felt around the outside to see if it was stuck in the bag itself, but found nothing. "Maybe it was just the corner of the basket," he concluded. "Sure felt sharper than that, though."

"Poor baby."

"You wanna kiss it better?" Brody leered.

"I'll pass." She unfolded the blanket and laid it out on the forest floor. "Have a seat." She grinned up at him.

Brody sat down and sprang back up quickly. "YEOWCH!"

"What is it?" Jess asked, but then laughed hysterically when Brody produced the pine needle that had jabbed his back end. "Guess that's been in there awhile, huh? You probably kicked it up while you were walking and it was stuck in your jeans the whole time." She rolled over on the blanket, still laughing.

Brody thought about retaliation, but then his stomach rumbled with hunger and he eyed the basket instead. "What'd you bring me to eat?"

KIM HARNES

Chapter Seven

Jess put the lens cap back on her camera and knelt next to Brody, who was asleep on the blanket. After watching him devour his ninth sandwich, she had spent an hour taking pictures of anything and everything that caught her eye: mountains, wildlife, dew covered leaves and moss-covered trees. There were insects resting in knotholes and birds resting in limbs. There were shadows casting bizarre silhouettes on the ground and clouds forming fantastic shapes in the sky.

Her quest for the perfect photograph was cut short, though, when Brody had suddenly bolted behind a thicket of trees to retch. She had gagged a bit herself when the hot smell of rejected salami and mustard wafted her way.

"You okay, Baby?" She stroked his hair away from the beads of sweat that formed at his temples.

He nodded weakly. "I don't know what's wrong."

"Could it be you ate too much?"

Brody mustered a feeble grin. "Never mattered before."

"You've got a point."

She continued to comfort him, but found herself sitting there helplessly as he jumped up once more and ran back behind the copse to expel the remainder of his lunch.

"Are you gonna be able to make it back?" she asked him as he lay down beside her for a second time and rested his head in her lap. She resumed caressing his forehead.

"I hope so. I just need to rest a little more." He closed his eyes and reached for her hand. A couple minutes later he was snoring softly.

****

"Mommy, can Brody stay for dinner?" Brody's nervousness ceased as he felt Jess's hand reach for his.

"Who the hell is Brody?" Amanda lit the end of her cigarette and took three long swallows from her drink.

"He's my friend from school. And he's on my baseball team."

"You made a friend*?" She cackled and slammed the empty glass on the table. The ice cubes clanked against the side, the liquid gone before they'd even had a chance to melt. "You hear that, Wes? Jessica has a friend."*

Brody watched and overheard as Wesley put his hands on Jess's shoulders and whispered in her ear, "She's just not feeling very well today, Jess," which Brody took to mean, "She's just drunk off her ass right now, Jess." But then he added, "Of course your friend Brody can stay for dinner."

Brody opened his eyes to the late afternoon sun. "How long was I out?" he asked groggily.

Jess was still beside him, his head still in her lap. "Couple hours. Feeling better?"

Brody sat up, took a personal record of his faculties, and stretched his long body as far as it would go. "I feel pretty freaking good, actually." And he did. "What time is it?"

"'Bout four."

"You ready to go home?"

Jess crinkled her nose. "At this point in time, I'm not really worried about whether or not *I'm* ready to go home. How are *you*?"

"I just told you I'm great."

Brody examined Jess's face as she contemplated their next move. "Let's stay here for a little bit longer," she said finally. "I'll take some more pictures while you rest."

"But …" Brody attempted to protest the fact that he was no longer incapacitated, but then realized he'd robbed Jess of a couple hours of daylight while she had tended to him. "Okay," he conceded.

Every once in a while he would catch a glimpse of her as she darted back and forth through the trees snapping more pictures. And every once in a while she'd come back to the clearing and switch out a lens from the black duffel bag. But then she'd quickly disappear again.

When she finally reappeared she was absolutely radiant. "You ready to go?" Her grin was wider than her face, if that were even possible. "I want to get these downloaded so you have time to get home before your dad calls lights out."

Brody jumped nimbly to his feet and began to pack the bag. "I can't wait to see what you took. As long as none of them are of me while I was puking."

"Don't worry." Jess smiled. "I was preoccupied with not getting vomit in my zoom."

"I had vomit in my zoom once. It's not as bad as it sounds."

In no time at all they were at the base of Peavine and headed toward Brody's car. The descent was easy. Brody had insisted on following Jess down the hill—not to keep her from falling, obviously, but so he could make sure wild animals didn't attack her from behind. She eyed him quizzically like she was pretty sure her behind was safe from every wild animal except Brody Campbell, but she let him have his way just the same.

Brody loaded the bag into his trunk once again, and they headed off to her house to print out the pictures of their escapade. The sun was just sinking behind the Sierras as they pulled into her driveway. The only light on in the house was the living room, and he figured Wesley was watching television and waiting for their arrival.

Jess wasted no time plugging everything in and the printer whirred moments later. Brody watched each picture slide into the tray upon its completion.

"So." Jess's dad appeared at the doorway and he leaned against the jamb. "Have fun?" The angry drawl in his voice led Brody to believe Jess had come home later than originally planned.

Jess turned and flashed a brilliant smile at her father. "Hi, Daddy!" She jumped up and gave him a hug. "You should come see all the pictures I took with my new camera! I'd have taken more, but Brody ended up getting a little sick to his stomach, and so I sat with him for a little bit, but I really think some of these are going to turn out really great."

Wesley's shoulders slackened and he entered the room. "A bit sick, huh?" He slapped Brody on the back with one hand and clamped his shoulder with the other. Brody figured he was relieved over the fact that he couldn't very well make a pass at his daughter while he was blowing chunks in the forest.

"Yes, sir," he answered.

"It was so sad, Daddy," Jess said empathetically. "He threw up and then he laid down and then he threw up and then he laid down. And then he fell asleep. I had to wait until he was able to make it back down the trail before we could leave."

"Well, I hope you're feeling better soon. Don't you have another game in a couple of days?"

"Tuesday. Yes, sir."

"Well, I hope you're up to it by then."

Brody was in the process of saying, "I'm sure I'll be fine, sir," but Wesley stepped between him and Jess.

"Let's see those pictures, J-Bird."

****

"Again? Really?" Jess glared at the stack of photos in her hand. Her dad had resumed watching television in the living room, leaving her and Brody alone.

"What's wrong?"

Jess handed a picture to Brody. "It's happening again." The unmistakable blob took up about a square centimeter in the bottom-middle. She rifled through more while Brody examined the one she'd given him. "And here are three more." She tossed them on the floor and sat back in her chair in disgust.

"This looks like … no, it can't be."

"What?" Jess sat back up with newfound interest. Brody had all four pictures in his hands, but held one separately.

"Doesn't this look like a brick wall?"

Jess snatched the picture from him and stared at it intensely. The overall image was of a blue bird extracting a nut from a pine cone amidst a background of deep green branches. To the right, however, was a small block that didn't belong. She pulled it closer so it almost touched her nose trying to see what Brody saw. It was a bit blurry, but it could definitely have been a wall of brick and mortar. "Can I see the rest?"

Brody passed her the other three photos and she eyed each one to see if she could make out anything else.

"More bricks here. Look." She handed another of the photos back to Brody and he nodded in agreement.

"I found another one, too." His voice was quieter – as though he was trying to talk around a lump in his throat. He was holding the larger stack of pictures. "This looks like someone's hand."

Jess froze. She didn't have to pull the photo close to see the delicate lines and pale color of a woman's arm and hand where it didn't belong inside the knothole of a large pinion pine. She remembered the other photos and retrieved them from the drawer. The chill ran up her spine when she saw one block that clearly showed a woman's high heel. "Oh, my gosh, Brody. Look at this."

"Wait a second." Brody took all the images from Jess and showed her one by one. "Each of the marks is in a different area."

"Yeah. So?"

"So, do you have any scissors?"

Jess didn't understand what Brody was doing, but she handed the shears over anyway.

"Can I have another piece of photo paper?"

She handed that to him as well, and then she winced inadvertently as the silver blades snipped apart her photograph.

"Got any tape?"

Jess finally understood his intentions. "How about a glue stick?" She opened another desk drawer and produced the cylindrical tube.

Brody grinned at her—that sheepish grin again. The one that made her insides jump.

After a few minutes, he showed her the finished product. "There are obviously a lot of pieces missing, but I think as you take more pictures, you'll be able to fill it in."

Brody had removed each of the squares and placed them on the new photo paper where they had appeared in the original piece. There were seven small blocks—each barely a half-inch square—positioned sporadically on a four by six canvas. Two of them actually fit side-by-side, and gave more life to the brick wall in the upper right corner.

"It's another picture." Jess didn't want to believe it, but the evidence was in her left hand. "They make another picture." Repeating the information only made her begin to feel a bit queasy, and she wondered if it was just the realization of it all, or if she were catching a touch of what Brody had exhibited up on Peavine. Still, she was intrigued by its mystery. "Let's look through the rest and see if we find more."

After they'd gone through every picture twice more, Jess was disappointed they'd only found three more blurbs, which were all randomly positioned and nondescript.

"I was hoping we'd get a better idea of what it was gonna turn out to be," she huffed.

"Guess you'll just have to take more pictures, then, huh? Think you can handle that?"

She smiled. "Oh, I'm pretty sure I can handle that."

KIM HARNES

Chapter Eight

Jess spent all day Sunday snapping pictures of anything she could think of: pictures of people, pictures of walls, pictures of furniture, pictures of pictures. She printed them all out three times each in an attempt to produce a smudge, and only ended up with one. More bricks.

And worse than that, she'd run out of photo paper.

Brody called around 2:00 and said he wasn't feeling very well again, but that he'd call her back about plans for that night. Jess filled him in on what she'd been doing all morning.

"So, it's not that big of a deal if you need to stay in bed," she said. "I'm gonna check with my dad and see if he'll get me some more paper."

"I've been thinking about that, Jess." Brody's voice was weak. "Maybe it's not such a good idea."

"What's not such a good idea?"

"Putting that picture together. It's ... well, it's creepy."

"I don't know why, Brody, but I need to see what it is. I need to know."

There was no response.

"Brody?"

Nothing.

"Brody, are you there?"

The line went dead.

Jess redialed Brody's number, but the line was busy. She tried again and again and she was about to ask her dad to drive her over there when the phone rang.

"Brody?" she panicked.

"Yeah, sorry."

"Oh, Baby, you sound *awful*."

He managed a pathetic laugh. "I had to go throw up and I didn't want to take you with me."

"Thanks for that."

"I'll call you later, okay? We'll still go out tonight."

"Not if you're still feeling like that."

"I'll be fine. I love you."

The line clicked before she had a chance to reciprocate.

"Hey, Dad?" She hollered to her father in the living room.

"Yeah, J-Bird?"

"I need more photo paper."

****

Brody propped himself up on the bathroom floor.

Just when he thought there was nothing else in his stomach to eject, out it came. He figured if he threw up one more time, his internal organs would turn inside out and wind up next to him on the tile.

He pressed his face against the cool porcelain, not even caring it was a toilet bowl, closed his eyes, and dozed.

Brody sat down on the school steps and wiped a tear off Jess's cheek, being careful not to touch the eye that had almost swollen shut. "You gonna be okay?"

"What am I gonna tell my dad this time?"

"You tell him what happened to me instead of what happened to you." Brody motioned to his own black eye. "Tell him you hit a foul ball and it came back at your face."

Her left hand was snared in the unkempt tresses at her temple. "Why does she hate me so much?" Jess sniffed hard, realized it wasn't enough, and wiped the rest of the snot on her sleeve.

Brody felt useless. He wanted to make her better, but didn't really know how. Eventually he put a clumsy arm around her shoulders and squeezed. It was apparently exactly what she needed, because she buried her face in his chest and wept while he held her until the bell rang.

Not the bell ringing. His cell phone ringing.

Brody was still curled on the bathroom floor when he answered. "Hello?"

"Are you still pukey? Do you need me to bring you some soup?"

The sound of Jess's voice always improved his well being, and when he sat up, he realized he no longer felt dizzy or nauseated. He stood cautiously just in case. "I think I'm okay, yes. Just woke up from a nap."

He wasn't about to tell her he'd fallen asleep hugging the toilet.

"I was going to let you off the hook and tell you that you didn't have to take me out tonight, but my dad didn't have the cash to get me more photo paper."

Brody didn't understand why he was so relieved about that. "Well, what do you want to do?"

"I was thinking—since you did spend the better part of the afternoon puking your guts out—maybe I could come over there and snuggle you on the couch while we watch a movie."

"Best idea ever."

"My dad already said he'd drive me over there," she said, answering his question before he'd had a chance to ask it. "Is five okay?"

He looked at his watch—quarter past four. He'd been asleep on the floor for two hours. "Five's perfect."

Brody continued to feel better and better waiting for Jess's arrival, and when he heard her dad's old Ford pickup in the driveway, his heart raced in his chest and he ran to the door to greet her.

"Hi, Handsome," she smirked. "I brought you something." In her right hand was a box of Saltine crackers. In her left hand was a family-sized can of Campbell's chicken noodle soup. "To make you feel better."

He said, "Thanks, Babe!" but was really thinking, "Great. More shit I can throw up later." He shook his head, forcing out the thought as well as the pang of anger at what he'd initially perceived to be Jess's inconsiderate gesture. He led her to the living room to curl up on the sofa, still confused over why he'd thought that to begin with. Jess didn't have a sardonic bone in her body.

"Are you okay?" Jess eyed him quizzically. "We don't have to do this if you're not feeling up to it."

"I'm fine!" he snapped. *What the—?* "I'm fine," he said again, softer this time.

Get a grip, Brody. What is the matter with you?

He sat down and rubbed the dull throb at his temple. "What are we going to watch?" He hoped he sounded a bit more like himself.

Jess seemed undaunted over Brody's erratic behavior. She flopped on the couch, then stole the remote control out of his hand and leaned against him. "Whatever I want." He didn't argue, and his anger soon subsided.

It hadn't been that long since they'd last been alone together, but Brody had forgotten how comfortable it was to just hold Jess. To lie there on the couch and not stir. To smell her hair and feel her subtle involuntary movements. To not have to make out, but just enjoy each other in silence. It was as natural as sleeping or breathing or being.

Jess laughed at the movie, and Brody had to feign interest. He didn't even know the title of what they were watching, let alone have any idea whatsoever of the plot. He was just content. Happy to be holding the girl he loved. The girl he wanted to spend the rest of his life with.

The girl he would do anything for.

****

Jess kissed Brody on the cheek as he held the door. "Thank you. I had fun."

She eyed his expression and figured he was disappointed at the lack of physical affection.

"I'd have kissed you better, but if you're contagious …"

The lines disappeared from his forehead and reappeared at his eyes as he morphed from glower to grin. "What, you don't want to holler for Ralph at the turd pool?"

She laughed at his disgusting yet accurate analogy. "It's not on my list of favorite things to do, no."

"You're working in the morning, right?"

"Yeah."

"Okay. I'll see you at school."

Jess quickly hugged Brody around his waist and jogged to her dad's truck as he pulled into the driveway.

Wesley put the truck in reverse as Jess snapped her seatbelt. "Did you have a nice time?"

"Yes, Daddy."

"His dad wasn't home?"

Always better to tell the truth. "No."

"What did you do?"

"Dad, we sat on the couch and watched a movie. Brody was puking all afternoon so I didn't even stick my tongue in his mouth."

Wesley's head snapped back as though he'd been struck. "I really don't appreciate your tone."

"Well, I really don't appreciate your insinuation."

"I wasn't insinuating anything."

"Really?" she said dryly. "The 'his dad wasn't home' question seemed like you were. Why did it matter if his dad was home or not?"

"Okay, so I was curious." He gripped the steering wheel tighter causing his knuckles to whiten. "But I wasn't accusing."

"I've already told you we haven't done anything."

"You're sixteen and he's seventeen, Jess. That's a status than can change on an hourly basis."

She heaved a sigh. This wasn't a fight she was going to win, nor was it a fight she wanted to get into. Her dad was convinced they were a pair of horny teenagers with overactive libidos. She figured he was probably right about that. In fact, she was pretty sure he was spot-on about that. But that didn't mean they'd acted upon it. It didn't mean they were going to act upon it.

Well, maybe eventually.

Chapter Nine

"Your dad told me you needed some of this, and I just happened to have some extra, so here you go." George handed over a large box.

She peered inside at the photo paper and ink. "Sweet, George! Thanks!"

"You're welcome. Gotta put that new camera to good use. It's mighty nice."

Jess beamed. "I know, right?"

"Ready to get to work?"

"Almost." Jess had thought long and hard about whether or not to tell George about the picture blotches and ask him if he'd ever heard of anything like that happening before. She had finally figured it couldn't hurt and let the story spill.

"Wow, Jess. That's interesting," he said when she finished. He scratched his bushy eyebrow, his fingers entangling in the long, coarse white hair. "I've heard of instances where people think they've captured images of ghosts or orbs, I've seen pictures atop other pictures because they were doubly exposed, and I've heard of a smudge appearing on the same spot on a picture because of a defective lens, but most of that went away when the world went digital. I've never heard anything like what you're talking about. It's kind of like a paranormal puzzle."

"That's exactly it."

"Well, you've got plenty of photo paper now, so keep it up. Who knows? Maybe the finished product will earn you a Pulitzer."

"Oh, geez. Another one?"

George chuckled. "Too many already?"

"Yeah. I'm running out of closet space."

"Well, let's put some miles on that camera. Misty and Molly should be on the set."

Blecch.

George must have seen her disappointment. "Oh, did I forget to give you this?" He winked and handed her several pieces of paper.

Jess took them and eyed them inquisitively, but then her eyes fell upon the words "Waiver and Release" and then "Montego Bay, Jamaica." Her mood improved exponentially. "George, this is only three weeks away."

"Yes. They moved it up. Corporate wanted to get the spread done ahead of time because they think there is potential for a calendar, which means they need it all by June 12th, which means *we* need everything by mid-May."

"I'm taking pictures of hot men that might end up in a calendar? How cool am I?"

George laughed again. "Let's take pictures of these hot twins, first, okay?"

Again, *blecch.*

****

"Are you coming over tonight? I took a bunch of pictures. Even snuck some on the bus."

Brody scratched the back of his head. He still wasn't positive the end result was worth it. Plus he was a little frightened, though he wasn't going to tell Jess that. "Are we trading off? You're coming to my practice, right?"

"Um ..."

Apparently she hadn't been planning on it. Ire bubbled his insides causing the hair to stand up on the back of Brody's neck. So much for the give and take in their relationship, he thought. After a few calming deep breaths that prevented him from saying something he would certainly regret later, he got control of his short fit of rage. "It's okay. I can still come over afterward."

She looked up at him and fluttered her eyelids. "Really?"

Brody's insides turned to mush. "Yes, really." He enveloped her in a bear hug and lifted her off the ground. After he set her back down, he added his own condition. "But you have to come to my game tomorrow."

"Let's not be silly," she teased. "Of course I'll be there for your game. I haven't missed one yet."

The rest of the morning was typical. Classwork assignments, homework assignments, note taking, note passing. He was careful not to eat too much at lunch— just in case his stomach decided to turn Exorcist again and cast out its contents like projectile pea soup. Fourth period came and went. Fifth period looked to be more of the same.

Until his nose began to bleed.

A lot.

"Oh, shit. Miss Wolfe, can I go to the nurse?"

Miss Wolfe put her hands on her hips and pivoted around to face him as she spoke. "I don't appreciate that lang—oh, shit! Someone help him to the nurse!"

He felt warmth on his sides as someone grabbed his waist and led him toward the door. Blood oozed around both of his hands, down his arms, and dripped off his elbows as he ineffectively attempted to stop the flow. Dark ruby droplets spattered the hallway like some B-rated horror flick.

"What the hell did you do, Brody?"

He recognized Carter Benson's voice and confirmed it was he who was guiding him to the nurse after he saw the torso beside him donning his trademark blue shirt. I duddo," he sputtered through the blood. "I didd't do addythig."

The front of his white t-shirt was almost completely scarlet when he finally stumbled into the infirmary. The nurse didn't flinch at his appearance—as though she'd seen a billion blood-soaked teenage boys. She pinched the bridge of Brody's nose and set him down on the stiff vinyl-covered cot. "Mr. Benson, there are towels next to my desk and ice packs in the cupboard up there. Please get me one of each." Her fingers were still firm against his sinuses, and he heard a cupboard close above him. The soft towel pressed against his face and soaked up what dribbled off his chin. "Now break the pack in half, shake it and hand it to me."

Several seconds later the blessed chill settled against the back of his neck. He hadn't even realized he'd been shaking until it began to subside.

"Okay, Mr. Campbell, are you able to tell me what happened?"

"Duthig," he groaned, his nose still tightly plugged by the nurse. "I jusd sdarded bleedig oudda dowhere."

"You weren't hit in the head or face?"

"Doh."

"Are you on drugs?"

"Huh?"

"You need to tell me the truth, Brody. Do you snort cocaine or heroin or methamphetamine?"

"Doh."

"Other inhalants like model glue or paint?"

"Doh. Duthig."

"Do you have allergies? Lots of sneezing? Any history of sinus problems?"

He shook his head no this time instead of talking around his nasal blockage.

"And your nose has never bled like this before?"

He shook his head once more. Some of the pressure released on one side of his nose as she checked to see if the flow had stopped, but then she clamped on again.

"Nice little gusher today, I'll say. Do you want me to call your dad?"

He shook his head a third time. "Baseball."

"Can't baseball wait one day?"

He was beginning to feel dizzy, but shook his head for the fourth and final time. "Gabe toborrow."

Her tone was curt. "And no practice the day before a game means no game." She had obviously dealt with school athletes in the past.

Brody finally nodded yes.

"Well, you're not going anywhere for the time being. You stay here and keep your nose pinched. I'll be back to check on you in a few minutes."

The weight shifted on the cot and he knew she'd gotten up. Brody continued to press the towel against his face, but still felt a bit woozy and he lay down on his side. The urge to vomit was growing steadily as the thick taste of blood trickled down the back of his throat.

He closed his eyes.

****

Jess burst through the door to see Brody lying on the cot, unable to see his face through the mostly-red-but-obviously-once-white towel. There was an ice pack on the pillow behind his head, and his shirt clung to his chest where the blood still had not dried.

"Holy hell, Baby." She dropped to her knees at his side and he pulled the towel away. The bleeding had stopped, but his face was whiter than his shirt—or what his shirt used to look like before he'd defiled it. Dried blood crusted his cheeks, chin, neck and hands and wound rust-colored streamers around his forearms. "You look awful." Tears stung the backs of her eyes.

Brody, with what appeared to be enormous effort, propped himself up on one elbow. "Wadda kiss be?"

Jess sat back on her heels and the corners of her mouth crept outward. "You jerk. Carter made it sound like you were dying in here."

"Jaditor busta got to the hallway with a bop, thed, 'cause I thought I was dyig, too."

"Are you better now, though?"

He pushed his fingers against his left temple. "Head hurts a little add I'b afraid to breathe oudda by doze for fear of adother blood flood, but I'b okay."

Jess got up, walked to the small sink, moistened a wash cloth, and went back to Brody. "You know you don't have to come over tonight if you're not up to it." She began to clean the dried blood off his face and neck. She knew it was selfish of her to want him there when he wasn't feeling so hot, but she still felt the burn behind her eyes again.

Brody must have seen the one tear that escaped. He gently took the cloth from her, found a clean spot, and wiped the trail off her cheek. "I'b fide."

Jess snorted. "Yeah, you *soud fide*."

Brody grinned causing the remaining crust on his cheeks to crack. "Okay, so I *will* be *fide* id a liddle while."

Jess took the washcloth from him again and rinsed it off in the sink. Pink water swirled around the basin and down the drain. She knelt beside him and resumed cleaning his face while he gazed into her eyes. "I'm just saying if you end up not wanting to come over, I'll understand. It's okay."

"Okay. I'll keep that id bide."

"Jessica?" The nurse entered, her overly starched uniform making a *voop* sound with each step she took. "Sixth period has started. Don't you think you should be there?"

"Yes, ma'am." Jess stood and kissed Brody on the forehead. "Guess I'll see you tonight."

He winked. His face was clean and his color was almost back to normal.

The nurse pulled a sheet off a perforated pad. "Here you go, Jessica. Just tell Miss Browning you saw me for a headache. No one has to know anything different, now, do they?"

Jess smiled wide and took the pass from her hand.

KIM HARNES

Chapter Ten

"Don't throw the ball to me, Dumbass! He's running to third!" Brody hurled the ball perfectly to Dave Towerey on the hot corner, but Mike Baker had already touched safely and adjusted his helmet. "What the hell were you thinking, Tom?" Brody jerked his mask back on and resumed his position behind home plate. "Come on, Boggsie! How the hell can you let Mike get a triple? He's a bench warmer, for Pete's sake! Put it in my glove this time." He punched the center of his mitt several times to show him where he wanted the ball.

The first one came in hard and fast and Ed Hatcher, the back up left fielder, swung at it ineffectively.

"That's the stuff, Pitch!" Brody tossed the ball back to Boggs and set up the next throw. After the wind up, the ball sailed in and ducked inside right at the last second tricking Ed and making him slice air with the bat.

That's two, Brody thought. *Bet he'll chase one low and away.*

But instead of low and away, the next pitch was over Brody's head and he ripped off his mask to chase it down. He found the ball at the backdrop, picked it up, and started to throw it to Boggsie at home plate, but he wasn't there and Mike scored easily from third. Brody looked around to see Boggs still on the mound, his shoulders slumped, his head down. Brody stormed toward him, the ball still clenched in his fist.

"If we play like this tomorrow McQueen is gonna *mutilate* us!" he bellowed. "You *cover* home plate when you throw a wild pitch and there's a runner on third, Boggs. Remember? Or did all the fundamentals of baseball skeet out of you with your last jack-off?"

"Brody, that's enough." Coach Traynor was jogging up behind him. "If I'm not mistaken, I'm still the coach of this team."

"Then coach it." He stuffed the ball in Boggsie's mitt and headed toward the dugout. He descended the steps, the clicking of his cleats and shin guards echoing off all three sides of the concrete enclosure, and threw his mitt against the back wall. Anger coursed through him, hot and wild in his veins.

"Son?" Coach Traynor's voice was behind him—apprehensive and, he thought, a bit scared.

His fury dissipated and he turned to face him. "I'm sorry, Coach. I don't know what got into me."

"Why don't you call it a day, Brody?"

"But ... No, Coach. It's okay. I'm okay." He reached for his mitt and began to walk by, but the coach put his hand on Brody's chest.

"I'm gonna let Pickle catch for the rest of the day. He needs the workout. You go home."

"Pickle?" Brody was dumbfounded. Pickle—nicknamed not because he had the uncanny ability to get himself into problematic situations, but because he had brought a jar of dill pickles to an away game which had broken in his duffel bag and subsequently stunk up the whole bus and stained his uniform a nice shade of light green—was certainly no baseball player. Larger around than he was tall, he could barely see the ball, let alone catch it.

"Yes. Pickle."

"Does ... does that mean he's playing tomorrow?" Brody knew the rule about practice just as the nurse had recited it to him.

"What am I, nuts? Hell no, he's not playing tomorrow. You showed up today. You practiced. You're just not … you're not *you* right now. I know what happened today at the nurse and maybe that has something to do with it. So I'm sending you home. It's my call today, so it's my call tomorrow whether or not you play. And I say you play."

Brody managed a half of a half of a smile. "Thanks, Coach."

Coach Traynor squeezed his shoulder. "Go get some rest, and we'll see you tomorrow."

Brody left the dugout and turned away from his teammates instead of toward them like he'd wanted to, and he didn't look back. He hated that baseball was being played and he wasn't a part of it. And apparently his teammates hated it as well. He could hear a few complaints and groans as Pickle suited up.

This was wrong. He should be with his team. He should be catching for practice. He should be there. Not Pickle.

Ire tried to rise in him again like the mercury in a thermometer, and he pushed it down with all the energy he could summon. Brody really didn't understand what was happening to him. He'd never been an angry person. Ever. And with all the lectures about respect his father had given him—what had been ingrained in him growing up—he certainly should *never* have talked that way to his coach. He knew to never be insolent toward someone of authority. He never had in the past.

He was always the one who took everything in stride. Brushed everything off. Let everything go. Never the one who flew off the handle.

So what was the difference? What was making him feel that way?

After a few more minutes of inner turmoil, he surmised his outburst must have had to do with the fact he'd been sick, and, therefore, a little more touchy than usual.

That had to have been it.

He'd never been one to get sick before, either.

At least one good thing had come of his leaving practice early. It meant he had more time with Jess, even if all they were going to do was put together that picture. That loathsome picture. His resentment stirred again. He didn't know why he hated it so much. It seemed like each of the images with a blemish on it vibrated within his fingers and made him feel weird, like the photos themselves were evil and just touching them would permeate his skin and make him evil, too.

But it was just ridiculous to think that.

****

Jess eyeballed her boyfriend inquisitively. "Are you gonna tell me?"

Brody heaved a tremendous sigh. "I'm just not feeling all that well. Sorry."

"Well, let's get to work. I've already found a few more pieces to our picture." She took his hand and led him to the computer, but wiped her palm on her pajama bottoms when she let go. His hands were never clammy. Eww. "Baby, are you sure you're up to being here?"

He was nonchalant. "Yeah. Why?"

She examined him a second time. He seemed fine. Didn't he?

She shrugged it off and headed to her computer. She had already separated what was once a large stack of photos into piles of "has a spot," "doesn't have a spot," and "could have a spot." She handed the "could have a spot" pile to Brody. "Here," she said. "Look at these and see what you think."

She thought just for the slightest second that Brody looked a little fearful over taking the pictures from her. But it passed quickly, like the flicker of a shadow across his face, and then he was all right again and shuffled through the stack.

Jess began to cut out what she knew to be obvious blocks of her picture and paste them into the new photo. There were six altogether. More bricks—boring. She already knew those were there. One looked like it could have been part of a light post, but there wasn't enough to tell. Another looked like it could have been red hair. A tennis shoe was off to the left in a position where it couldn't possibly coincide with the hand already there, so she assumed there were at least two people in the photo.

"Here are two more," Brody said quietly.

"Sweet!" Jess snatched them out of his hand exuberantly and went at them with the scissors, not caring anymore that she may be slicing apart some priceless work of art. She did notice, though, that the one she was demolishing was one of the strange, bald, cursing druggie from the bus that she had taken without his knowledge or permission. What she had initially thought may or may not have been a spot was in the window behind him, and it was difficult to see if it was actually something outside the bus, which was blurred by their movement, or an actual piece of her puzzle. "Thanks, Baby! This fits great. I think it's more to the lamp post. See?"

Brody seemed to flinch away from the photo when she held it toward him, but he then examined it and agreed. "Yeah. Looks like it."

"Can you look through this pile and see if I missed anything?" She passed him the "doesn't have a spot" pile.

"Sure."

As Brody rifled through the new mass of snapshots, Jess pretended to peruse through more, but kept him in the corner of her eye. He wasn't right. She couldn't put a finger on what it was, but it was definitely something. And it was something more than just his being sick. She'd spent enough time around Brody Campbell to know his inner workings, and his foreboding expressions. She knew he thought this whole picture thing was odd, and she didn't exactly disagree with him, but he really seemed frightened about the unknown where she was excited about figuring the whole thing out.

"What do you think about this one?" Brody's voice knocked her out of her thoughts and she took the picture of the graffiti-covered bus stop canopy. "Here, see?" He pointed to a splotch that didn't belong within the ornately drawn name of the hoodlum-slash-artist who had besmirched the Plexiglas awning.

"Nice! I missed that one. See why I keep you around?" She kissed him on the forehead and he smiled. She attacked this one with the scissors as well, snatched the glue stick off the desk, and added it to the rest of the fragments.

They went like that for another half hour and found three additional pieces. Jess had been applying the last of these to the paper when Brody yelped. She whipped around in her chair to see him gripping his left hand in his right, blood dripping from the wound in his palm onto the photo at his feet.

"Paper cut," he said between clenched teeth.

"Holy crap!" Jess jumped up to get some tissue and almost threw the box into Brody's lap. That was an awful lot of blood for just a paper cut.

When Brody had wrapped his hand in enough tissue to suppress the flow, Jess focused on what had caused him to bleed in the first place. She bent down and retrieved the picture off the floor. Blood oozed thick over the centimeter-sized block she'd somehow missed.

"Maybe we should just stop for now." Brody winced as he put pressure on the cut.

Jess didn't pay any attention. She wiped off what she could, cut out the required section, attached it to the still unfinished product, and stared at Brody, her mouth agape.

"What? What is it?" Brody still clenched his injured hand in wads of tissue.

The picture shook in her hand as she passed it to Brody and a hot tear streaked down her face. "It's my mother."

KIM HARNES

Chapter Eleven

The quest to finish the photograph over, Brody held his distraught girlfriend on the couch. Every once in a while he'd catch her twirling the hair at her left temple, and when he did, he'd gently touch her elbow to remind her. She would look up at him with red-rimmed eyes, smile halfheartedly, and lower her hand to her lap.

He had known that picture was bad. He had known nothing good would come of it. And now he had the proof.

It was *her.*

Fury flashed through him just thinking about her. He knew what she had done to Jess before he came around, and he knew what she had done to Jess in the two years before she took off. He had been there for some of it—watched as she shoved her down, berated her, and belittled her. *"What's Brody gonna do? Tell on me?"* she had shrieked once. Right after that she had thrown what was left of her drink, which wasn't much, into Jess's face with enough force to leave a small mark on her forehead from an ice cube.

"Why can't we just run away, Brody?" Jess's tear-streaked face looked up into his, pleading. "Why can't we just get away from her?"

He didn't know what to say to her. He didn't know what to do. "We can't just leave, Jess. We're only kids. Where are we going to go?"

She sniffled and wiped her nose on the back of her hand leaving what resembled a slug trail up her forearm. Then she smiled, the tip of her tongue visible from the gap where her tooth had fallen out. "I know where we can go."

She took Brody by the hand and led him to the back yard. The afternoon breeze sent a spiral of leaves across the mostly dead lawn as they walked toward the rickety plywood playhouse.

"This is my castle." She motioned to the dilapidated shack and then air-curtsied, pretending her dirty shirt and ripped jeans were an elegant gown.

"I see, fair princess." Brody played along and bowed low, smiling his own missing-tooth smile.

"You don't need to worry about the evil witch finding us here," she said matter-of-factly. "I have a pet dragon and he'll eat her up."

Brody took Jess's hand away from her left temple once more, and this time clasped it in his as he kissed her where the hair was most tangled. Jess snuggled closer, so he kissed her again at the base of her ear. Hearing her breathing accelerate, he moved his lips down her jaw line slowly until she turned into him, wrapped an arm around his neck, and met his next kiss with her own.

They entangled themselves on the couch and even though he usually shied away from Jess when he was … aroused, this time he held her closer and kissed her more deeply. He wanted her right then and there. All thoughts of feeling ashamed over his past misconduct aside, he let a hand wander upward. This time, though, Jess was quick to return it to a safe zone.

He wasn't sure if she would continue to resist him for much longer, but he wasn't able to find out as keys jingled in the lock announcing the imminent entrance of Jess's dad through the front door.

They both sat up quickly and Brody ran his fingers through his hair as Jess adjusted her blouse. They pretended to be watching television as Wesley entered the room. "Hey, kids." He set his keys on the small table next to the sofa.

"Hi, Daddy!" Jess smiled brightly despite the glumness of her mood just a few short minutes ago. "George gave me the waivers today, so if you can sign them I can get them back to him when I go to work on Wednesday. It's three weeks away!"

Brody slumped in his seat. Oh, yeah. She was leaving. He listened to the remainder of the conversation with disinterest.

"Okay, J-Bird. Guess I have to try to fish your passport out of the attic."

"I have a passport?"

"Yeah. We got you one when you were nine. We were going to take a family trip right before … right before your mom left."

"Oh. I don't remember."

"I'll see if I can find it tonight."

"Thanks, Daddy."

"How late is Brody staying?"

Brody's head turned toward the mention of his name. "Seven-twenty, sir." He cleared his throat. "I'm supposed to be home by seven-thirty."

"Another game tomorrow, right?"

"Yes, sir."

"You get a good practice in today?"

Brody thought about lying, but then thought better of it. "Only so-so. I haven't really been feeling well the past couple days, so Coach let me out early."

Wesley chuckled. "I guess he didn't want you puking in your helmet, eh?"

Brody relaxed a bit. "Guess not." He hated that he always felt Wesley knew when he'd just pawed his daughter, but was relieved again to think he wouldn't suspect him of sexual misconduct if he were sick.

"Well, I'm sure you'll do fine tomorrow. You always do."

"Thank you, sir."

"No problem." He turned and left the room.

"That was a close one." Jess poked Brody in the side. "Ya freaking octopus!"

Brody grinned and looked away, the heat in his face intensifying again. Then he turned back toward her and stared into her eyes. "One of these days you may let me round second base," he teased. "And I'll keep trying until you do."

"You're hopeless."

"No, see, there's where you're wrong. I'm hope-*ful*."

****

Jess was halfway up the attic stairs when her dad began to descend. "Did you find it?" she asked as her feet hit the floor.

"Yeah." He grunted as he lowered himself down the rickety ladder. He reached the bottom with a final grumble, dropped two large and dusty suitcases at his feet, and took the small black book out from between his teeth. After he handed it to Jess, he folded the steps back into the door and raised it until it hid itself in the ceiling, the rope cord swaying back and forth just inches above his head.

Jess fingered through the pages of her passport and huffed in protest when she saw the picture. "Dad, can we get a new one?"

"What? No. Why?"

"Cause this is a picture of me when I was a little kid." She held it out so he could examine it, but he looked away. "And what's that all over my face? Gross."

"Well, yeah. I told you we had these done a while ago. I think you had just come from a game in the rain. You were always dirty when you were younger, J-bird. Tomboys usually are. But passports are good for ten years and they're really expensive, so that one will have to do."

She made a noise like a *tsk* and a *psshhh* and then said, "Fine."

Wesley frowned at his daughter. "I can still refuse to sign the waivers."

Jess stood still. He'd denied her privileges in the past when she'd complained, and took his threat seriously. "This is fine, Daddy. I'm sorry." She held her breath and prepared for the worst.

His eyes were mere slits as he presumably examined his daughter's sincerity. Then he smiled. "Can you help me with the suitcases?"

Jess slowly exhaled the gulp of air and white spots popped before her eyes. She blinked them away and took the handle of the smaller of the two bags, which she dragged down the hallway toward her bedroom.

"This enough for your trip?" Her dad set his case down on her floor against the wall.

Jess covered the giggle with her hand. "Um, Dad, I think this is enough for me to be gone for a month and a half, not four days!"

"I thought teenage girls had to pack their entire bedroom, bathroom, and kitchen just to leave for the afternoon."

"You're confusing me with a *normal* teenager." She poked her dad in the side. "You know, the frilly, high-maintenance girls with lots of make-up that change their clothes four times a day, have spray-on tans and manicures, and have a drawer full of hair products."

"You're not one of those?" He tried to tickle her side, but she dodged his grasp.

"No, thank goodness."

"Good." He put his hands on his hips. "I guess I'll leave them both in here just in case, and if you only need one, I'll take the other one back up to the attic when you leave."

The last word lost a little emphasis, and Jess figured Brody wasn't the only one who didn't want her to go. She hugged her dad tight. "I'll be back." She didn't know why she felt she needed to say that—as if she needed to reassure him of her return because he was somehow expecting her to take off and leave forever as her mother had.

"I know, J-Bird." He sighed and returned her squeeze. "I know."

****

Brody answered the phone with a smile. "You miss me already?"

"I have to tell you something."

"Hang on a second. I gotta get the door open."

Brody's dad confronted him as he entered the house. "Coach told me you left practice early. If you're too sick to finish practice, you're too sick to see your girlfriend."

Brody's fury began at his fingertips, sizzled up his arms, and burned hot in his face. He dropped his gear in the hallway and pivoted curtly to face his father. "I didn't leave practice early because I was sick. Don't hurt yourself jumping to conclusions, *Dad.*" Brody's dad recoiled and took a step back as if he thought his son might hit him. Brody felt nothing but white-hot anger so intense his skin tingled and his vision blurred. "You won't keep me from Jess no matter how hard you try." He spoke calmly and clearly and he could sense the fear in his father's wide eyes. "I play baseball for me, get it? For me and not you. Because I love baseball. You can't play anymore and that kills you. You messed up your own life and made my mother watch and it killed her, too. You want your youth back and you can't have it, so you're trying to live vicariously through me and it eats you up inside. You want to be me so badly you can taste it. But you were never as good as you thought you were."

His dad just stared, visibly frightened.

"You go to my games and picture yourself on the mound, don't you, Dad? And all the while you're telling yourself how you'd have done it differently. How you'd have gotten just a little more curve ... How you'd have thrown it a little bit harder. Convincing yourself that you were better. Fooling yourself into thinking you were the best. But the truth is you weren't anything more than a second-rate pitcher on a third-rate team."

"What's that have to do with …"

"And it's the same thing with Jess, isn't it? When you see me with Jess do you miss Mom? When you look at us together don't you think maybe if you'd have been more attentive—if you'd have been more affectionate—if you'd have been more *anything* with her she may still be alive?"

"That's enough." His dad was trying to sound stern, but his voice squeaked with fright. Brody had never spoken to him this way.

And he wasn't finished.

"No, it's *not* enough." Brody felt spit fly from his lips and watched his dad flinch when it sprayed his cheek. "You have been on my ass every day of my life. Walk like this. Eat like this. Throw the ball like this. Go to bed now. Get off the phone. Do it my way. Get up at the ass crack of dawn and go to bed before the streetlights come on. Do all your homework and eat all your vegetables and grow big and strong. Practice at school and practice at home and practice in your head until all you can think about is what's been crammed into it. Well, I'm sick of it. And I'm done with you. So from now on, leave me the hell alone."

He turned and ran up the stairs.

"Brody?"

His phone was still in his hand, and the anger released its grip when he thought of Jess on the other end of the line. "Oh, Jess, I'm sorry."

"You just said all that to your dad?"

"Yeah."

"Was he in the room at the time?"

Brody chuckled. "Yeah."

"Daaaaaaaaamn."

"I know, right? So, what did you want to tell me?"

"How do I know you won't bite my head off?"

Brody smiled at her joke. "Trust me."

"I just wanted to tell you that I love you, but I guess I'll just leave you the hell alone."

He ignored the playfulness in her voice and wiped at the fresh flow of blood that began to trickle from his nose. "Don't *ever* leave me the hell alone, Jess Waterford. *Ever.*"

Chapter Twelve

"Did you see it, Daddy?" Jess's hat was askew as she stood at the opening of the dugout and flashed a toothless grin at her dad. "My first home run ever!"

"I did see, J-Bird. That was amazing!"

"I really knocked the crap out of it, didn't I?"

Wesley uttered an embarrassed giggle and looked around to see if anyone else had heard his daughter's use of language, which, though spoken with pure innocence, was not exactly typical of a nine-year-old girl. Then he turned back toward her and returned her smile. "Yes you did. I'm so proud of you."

"Did mom see?" she asked hopefully. "Is she proud of me, too?"

Jess's dad glimpsed at Amanda in the stands, uninterested and indifferent, and turned back to Jess. "Of course she saw. And yes, she's proud of you, too."

"Really?" Jess's smile spread across her face as far as her little mouth would allow. "She really is?"

He smiled and tugged on the brim of her cap, straightening it on her head. "She really is." He turned her head to one side and then the other, observing the bruises on her neck—four marks about two inches long on one side, a smaller, darker spot on the other. "What happened to your neck, J-Bird?"

Jess flinched. Think fast. *"I ..."* Can't say Mommy did it. *"Um ..." Where else would bruises like that come from, but the right hand of Amanda Waterford, constricted around her throat? What else could cause the perfect imprint of four fingers and a thumb? Her mind whirred with possibilities. A bicycle mishap? A slip in the bathtub? A fall off the bed? She thought back to the bruises Brody had had on his neck and remembered* where they had come from. *"The tire swing,"* she said finally. *"I was messing around on the tire swing and slipped off and the tire got me here ..."* she pointed to one side of her neck, *"... and then the rope got me here,"* and she referenced the other.

He didn't look entirely convinced.

Amanda must have noticed Wesley's examination of their daughter and she traipsed down the wooden bleachers in her high heels and made it to his side in record time. *"I want to go,"* she announced. *"It's dirty here."*

Wesley stood, his attention no longer on his daughter's injuries, which was, judging by her smug expression, her intention. *"But it's only the third inning."*

Amanda gave Wesley an I-don't-care-what-you-think-because-we're-doing-what-I-want-anyway sort of look and put her hands on her svelte hips, as if daring him to challenge her authority.

"Well, I'll just take you home and come back for the rest of the game."

The enormous feeling of triumph that had ballooned inside Jess over hitting her first inside-the-park homerun deflated at the departure of her parents. She watched them walk away, hand-in-hand.

Jess turned back toward the dugout.

"Great hit, Jess!" Brody joined her as soon as she sat at the end of the bench.

Jess was inconsolable. *"It was okay."*

"Okay? Even if Jake didn't muff that throw to second you still woulda had a triple, I bet. It rolled all the way to the fence."

Jess sniffled loudly.

"What happened?" Brody looked into the stands. *"Where'd your mom and dad go?"*

He always knew. "They left. Mom wanted to go home cause she was gettin' dirty. Dad said he'd be back, though. After he took her home."

"You didn't tell your dad about your neck and what she did, did you?"

Jess shook her head vigorously from side to side. Brody was the only one she told. Ever.

Brody began to strap on his shin guards. "Well, get your mitt ready," he said. "Henry Nose-Picker Pickering is a pitch away from our third out."

His mention of her nickname for Henry made her smile, and she pulled her mitt out from under the bench. She couldn't be thinking about her mom, anyway. They did have a game to win, after all.

Jess pulled her hand out of the ensnared mess of hair on the left side of her head. Her mind continued the dream with her own recollection of what had happened afterward.

Her dad didn't come back to watch the game as he had said he would. She checked the bleachers for him so often she thought she'd given herself whiplash. She'd had an extraordinary game, despite her frame of mind, including two more extra-base hits and making the winning catch on a comebacker. She attributed much of that to Brody, who kept her mood light and praised her accomplishments.

After the game, several parents had offered to give her a ride home so she wouldn't have to wait in the impending thunderstorm, but Jess knew the consequences for not being where she was supposed to be when she was supposed to be there.

She waited in the parking lot as the sky opened up and poured upon her and her duffel bag, thankful at least the rain hid her tears. The sky had darkened with the storm clouds as well as the lateness of the hour.

Finally, despair devouring her with each minute that ticked by, a pair of headlights appeared and the car pulled up beside her. She realized her mother was driving when the tip of her cigarette glowed orange against her face.

The motor churned as the window lowered. "What are you waiting for? Get in."

Jess was frozen with fear and the rain continued to come down, soaking through her clothes and dripping off the end of her nose. Where was her dad? Why hadn't he come for her? Lightning flashed in the distance, quickly followed by a loud crack.

"Listen, you little shit. Either you get in this car, or I drive off without you and consider you a runaway. No skin off my ass either way."

And still, Jess could not move.

The car door opened and Amanda flicked her cigarette onto the pavement. It made a hiss as the rain extinguished the ember at the tip. "Get in the car, you disgusting little troll!" She had reached Jess in two giant steps with her long legs and dug her French manicure into the flesh on her shoulders as she wrestled her toward the car.

Jess's duffel bag dragged along behind her and it made a sick sound as it slid across the wet asphalt.

"Hurry *up!*"

Her mother's foot hit her square in her lower back knocking her to the ground and causing her head to hit the open car door.

Jess's world went black.

****

As soon as she climbed into his car, Brody sensed Jess's angst, scooted over to her, and wrapped his arms around her as tightly as they would go. She instantly broke down and sobbed against his shoulder. "One of these days we'll get the hell out of this town and leave everything behind." The resentment toward Jess's mother welled up in him as he stroked his girlfriend's hair and let her cry it out.

"I'm so sorry, Brody."

He laughed. "What are you sorry for? That your mom was Satan's babysitter?"

Jess pulled away and looked at him remorsefully. All he could do was take in the beauty of her face, flush with emotion, and her eyes teary, but bright and lucid. "No, because it happened again and you have a game today. You need to be worried about playing and not about me."

Brody drew her back into his chest. There would be plenty of time to worry about the game later.

And worry he did as the day crept on. He began to think about his abysmal practice the day before. He worried they would all play horribly and would lose on miscues and errors. And he worried he'd lose his temper again.

In fact, that's what he agonized over the most. He didn't like being angry. Neither how it made him feel, nor how it made him act. But somehow lately the fury soared in him so quickly and completely until it just took over leaving the quieter, more rational Brody in its wake.

His anguish was not only over how he'd treated his coach and his teammates, but also how he'd disrespected his father. He had no idea where those horrible words had come from. And the worst part was his dad hadn't crossed his path since that episode so he could apologize and take it all back.

Brody's temple began to pound with each beat of his heart and he tried to push the pain away with his fingertips. Try as he might, the throbbing continued to grow and he unwillingly exhaled an agonized moan.

"Are you okay, Brody?" Miss Wolfe, who probably didn't want to witness a second apocalyptic episode in as many days, approached his desk.

Her voice was barely audible to Brody. The pain had grown rapidly and it was now so intense it pulsed bright screams across his forehead and down his neck. "Oh, God," he mumbled and pressed his face against the desk. "Oh, God, what is happening to me?" He stood, but his head protested and his vision blurred. "Make it stop. Please make it stop." He pleaded to anyone who would listen to put him out of his misery. His head shrieked again. Or did that noise come from him? "Please," he begged. "Can't somebody please make it stop?" Brody stammered and stumbled aimlessly, positive his head would soon explode and end his suffering. His leg banged into someone's desk. He didn't feel it, but it was hard enough to move it several meters across the floor. He vaguely heard someone protest as he stepped on her foot.

"Jessica." Someone whispered her name. He didn't know who'd done it or where they were but it sounded as if it were inside his own throbbing head. "Jessica." Was he calling for her? Was someone going to get her? Would she be coming to help him? And could she make him better?

Just when he thought the pain couldn't get any worse, another squeal of hurt detonated within his left eyebrow and buckled his knees. "Can't someone please make it stop?" He implored one last time to anyone who may still be within earshot. He crawled across the linoleum, oblivious to anything but the searing sting like a white-hot sword twisting in his temple.

Exhausted and spent, he curled into the fetal position on the floor and waited for death to come and mercifully take him away, because he was sure that was the only thing that would release him from this torture.

His skull opened and whiteness entered.

The warm, bright light comforted him and he reached for it.

"Jessica," his head whispered again.

KIM HARNES

Chapter Thirteen

"Jessica?"

She sat up and wiped a small stream of drool off her cheek, her nightmare about Brody fading with her fear. "Sorry."

Mrs. Voorhies, her voice softening as she laid a hand gently on Jess's arm. "Jess, they've taken Brody to the hospital."

"What?" The fear returned immediately with the realization that it wasn't a dream, and what she had seen had really happened to him. She walked to the office in a daze her mind wandering to the still unfinished picture at home. She half wanted to go home now that she didn't have to go to Brody's baseball game so she'd have extra time to work on getting it completed. She had a new stack of flawed pictures to dissect and reassemble. And if her dream was right, Brody wasn't even conscious and probably wouldn't even know she was there.

She shook the thought out of her head and mentally scolded herself for even considering *not* going. That was absurd. Of course she was going to go. She dialed the seven numbers to her dad's phone and waited impatiently for him to come get her, and she jumped out of the truck before it came to a full stop at the Emergency entrance.

Knowing she shouldn't run inside the hospital, she slowed to a brisk walk from the entrance doors to the information counter. "What room is Brody Campbell in, please?"

The receptionist typed his name into the computer. "Campbell, Brody," she ticked off robotically. "Room 228. Elevators are down the hall to your left.

Take it to the second floor, exit the elevator and turn right."

The hallway was too long and the elevator was too slow, but she eventually reached his room. Brody was hooked up to a labyrinth of wires and tubes. The television was on, and Jess noted thankfully that it was just loud enough to drown out the beeping, buzzing, and whirring of the machinery. She approached the side of his bed and took his hand in hers. An IV was taped to the top of it pushing clear fluid into his veins and a clothespin-type device pinched his index finger monitoring his pulse and oxygen level.

Despite everything else, he just looked like he was sleeping.

"He's on a lot of medication." His dad's voice startled her. She hadn't noticed him when she entered the room. "He … he's been in a lot of pain."

Jess looked at him and he turned away—probably ashamed of his tears. Or maybe even ashamed he had exhibited any emotion at all, as she had never seen him do that before. Not even when his wife died. "What happened?"

"We're not sure, actually. Still waiting on some test results." He began to pace around the hospital room. "I guess he made quite a scene in class. They even had to sedate his teacher."

Jess felt a pang of sympathy for poor Miss Wolfe, who was always a little skittish, anyway.

"He's had a CT Scan and some X-rays and some blood work."

"Well, how long until we know anything?" Jess had barely gotten the words out when Brody gently squeezed her hand causing her heart to beat practically out of her chest. "He … I think he's waking up."

His dad approached the other side of the bed and gripped the metal rail.

"Jess?" Brody's head turned toward her and he winced a little, but his eyes fluttered open and fixed on hers.

"I'm here, Brody."

"It hurts."

"Okay, Baby. We'll get someone for you."

Brody's dad had already turned to exit the room and returned a half-minute later with a nurse in cartoon-laden scrubs.

"Hi there, Handsome!" the nurse chirped. "What can I do for you today?"

"Don't want anything," he said. "Just water."

"Water. Got it. Anything else?"

Brody slowly shook his head no and the nurse flitted out the door.

Jess protested. "But you said your head hurt."

"But you're here and I want to stay awake while you're here." He squeezed her hand again. "The pain medication knocks me out."

Jess managed a smile. Though she wanted him to take something to feel better, she knew he wasn't going to give in.

"I thought …" His throat was obviously dry and the nurse popped in with a cup of ice chips. He let one melt on his tongue and then he continued. "I heard someone calling you, so I knew you'd be here when I woke up."

"You heard someone calling me?"

"Yes. When my head started hurting so badly. I knew they were going to get you and you'd be here."

She figured it must have been the medication talking, so she just let it go.

Brody's dad approached the bedside again. He glanced briefly at Jess, and then turned around to, once again, hide his pained face.

Brody turned back toward Jess, flinching a bit at the movement. "I'm missing my baseball game for the first time since … ever."

Jess giggled. "I guess it's a good thing Pickle got in a little practice yesterday, huh?"

Brody groaned. "We're doomed."

As they continued to chat about the demise of the North Valley's High School baseball team with Pickle at the helm, Jess couldn't help but notice some of the color had returned to Brody's face. "You almost look like you're feeling better."

Brody blinked and looked as though he was thinking about it. "I kinda am." He blinked a few more times, shook his head from side to side and up and down, stretched his long body from head to toe, and grinned a well-whaddya-know grin. "I kinda *really* am."

The lightness that filled the air changed palpably as the doctor entered the room, his crisp, white coat and furrowed brow just reeking of doom and gloom. He had films in his hands, and Mr. Campbell met him at the foot of the bed while Jess and Brody strained to hear.

"It's not good, Mr. Campbell. But we're not sure it's all that bad, either."

Brody's dad looked at him curiously. "I'm pretty sure you're using layman's terms, Doctor, but I'm also pretty sure I still don't understand you."

"Well, to tell you the truth, we see something, but we're not quite sure what it is."

Mr. Campbell stiffened. "You don't know what it is?"

"No, sir. It's nothing we've ever seen before." He took the images he'd brought, flipped the switch on the box on the wall, and pressed them up against the lighted screen. "We know it's not a tumor, and we know it's not an aneurysm, and we know it's not hydrocephalus."

"Well, then what *is* it?" Brody's dad was becoming impatient.

"As I said, we don't know." The doctor indicated a large and misshapen cloudy mark on the left side of the scan. "This is contrary to anything we've ever seen in medical science. It's obvious there's *something* there. We just don't know what it is. So, unfortunately, we don't know if it's operable, if it's cancerous, or if it's permanent or temporary. Your son may experience nosebleeds and headaches forever if this doesn't dissipate, or it may grow and cause him more problems, or it may go away and he'll be perfectly fine. We just … don't … know."

Brody and Jess looked at each other, and then back at the doctor.

"So, what does this mean for my son right now?" Mr. Campbell asked.

"We'd like to keep him for a few days for observation. We'll do a couple more CT scans and monitor the—the whatever it is in his skull, and hopefully we can come up with a prognosis."

"The 'whatever it is' in his skull." Mr. Campbell snorted his disapproval. "Four years of college, four years of medical school, two years of residency, and my guess is since you're a Neurologist you had more schooling on top of that, and all you have for me is the 'whatever it is' in his skull. Nice."

The doctor puffed up defensively and his tone became snappish. "Our other option is to cut his skull open and find out what it is that way, but we'd rather not take such invasive measures at this time."

Brody's dad cowered a bit. "Monitoring him is fine for the time being."

"That's what I thought." He exited the room leaving the three of the remaining occupants to stare after him in dumbfounded silence.

****

Brody stared at the ceiling and waited for the medication to course through his bloodstream. He wasn't in much pain, and he'd objected to the syringe, but the doctor had insisted. The nurse had insisted. Jess had insisted. And then his dad had insisted.

He was pretty sure Jess was going to be leaving soon, and she promised to come back right after school the next day and tell him everything she could gather about the baseball game. That felt like an eternity to him. But, unfortunately, he had enough to keep him occupied in the hospital. He'd had another CT scan, and a half hour later the doctor came in, said something inaudible to his dad, and then scheduled another. He was due for that in about a half hour, and he was thankful he'd be fairly comatose after his latest elephant-sized dose of morphine, which, he noticed, was finally beginning to tingle his fingers and droop his eyelids.

"Brody?"

He blinked groggily at his dad. "Yeah?" His mouth was dry and sticky.

"I'm going to drop Jess off on my way home, but I'll be back first thing in the morning. The doctor is going to call me with the results of your next CT scan."

"Mmmmkay."

"I ... Good night."

"G'night."

Brody was fairly sure they had left, though he didn't see them go. The tingling in his fingers spread up his arms and throughout his body, and his eyelids were too heavy to keep open.

He gave in willingly.

****

Jess pasted a block on her photo and looked at the digital clock on her desk right as the time clicked to 1:52. Her dad had told her to go to sleep hours ago, but she was pretty sure that wasn't going to happen. She was on a roll.

The brick wall was close to being complete, as was the lamp post. She'd added quite a bit more to her mother and she was pretty sure there was at least one other person, as she'd pieced together a pair of legs and one elbow.

She was tired. She knew she should go to bed. But something compelled her to continue. She only had four more defective photos left to cut out and affix to her canvas, and not even sleep deprivation would keep her from it.

She painstakingly snipped and glued, snipped and glued.

And then she stopped cold.

The image of her mother had become more absolute – more evident of what it really showed, and Jess trembled at the sight of it. Blood covered the front of her mother's shirt, trailed down her body, and pooled on the ground reflecting the light from the lamp post in an eerie red glow. She stood there with a dumbstruck expression, her fiery red hair matted to her head, her arms straight down at her side, her eyes unfocused.

Jess was horrified over the realization of the object she held in her hand.

Jess wasn't just piecing together a photo of her mother.

She was piecing together a photo of her mother's murder.

Jess grasped the hair at her left temple and screamed in fear.

****

At St. Mary's Hospital, the patient in room 228 put his hand to his left temple and screamed in pain.

Chapter Fourteen

Brody was sick of the hospital.

Not only that, he was sick of having CT scans, which were now ordered every hour of the day for some unknown reason no one would talk to him about. He was sick of not being able to wear his favorite jeans and t-shirt and ball cap. He was sick of medication and IV's and hospital food.

And most of all, he was sick of not seeing Jess.

Now Saturday morning, she hadn't come to see him since he was admitted to the hospital Tuesday afternoon and he had no idea why. He'd never gone four days without her since they'd met. She hadn't returned his calls or texts, and, frankly, he was beginning to get a little pissed off.

Temper, he reminded himself again.

His anger was getting more and more intense and more and more frequent. His doctors all told him it "could be but they're not sure if it is" a result of his "whatever it is" in his skull, which, of course, pissed him off more.

Five days of tests and all they could tell him and his dad was nothing was conclusive. He'd been poked and prodded and jabbed and scanned and X-rayed. He'd peed in a cup, pooped on a card, and bled into vials. When he thought they'd done every test imaginable, they did them all again.

He was weary and stressed and stressed over being weary and sick and tired and tired of being sick.

And all of it made him angry.

Anytime someone entered the room, his heart leapt in the hopes it was Jess. And it sank just as quickly when he realized it wasn't. And the resentment overwhelmed him. The doctor came in to check on him just after his tasteless breakfast and he, of course, had no more news, but advised Brody he was scheduled for several more tests that afternoon.

"More tests?" he objected. "How many more tests can I possibly do? Why don't you just go back and look at your old tests!"

But the doctor was adamant that it was all for his own good and if he refused to take the tests they'd never figure out what was wrong with him and he'd never get better, and didn't he want to get better?

At this point, Brody wasn't sure *what* he wanted, except for two things. He knew he wanted to be out of the hospital, and he knew he wanted Jess.

"Time to get your cat scanned, Handsome!" The chipper nurse entered the room beaming a smile and pushing a wheelchair. "Hop on in!"

Brody heaved a sigh and got up. He was thankful, at least, that he was allowed to wear his own pajamas after numerous complaints to anyone that would listen that he was really done with mooning all the nurses every time he had to get up. Although he was pretty sure most of the nurses (and maybe even one of the doctors) weren't all that upset over seeing his butt, sometimes he did catch a draft.

"There ya go!" she chirped as he sat down. "Ready?"

Not waiting for his response, she wheeled him through the now familiar maze of hallways and elevators until they reached the radiology wing. She steered him into the small, white room where the machine was already droning.

"You know the drill. I'll be right outside." She flipped up the foot pedals and allowed him to move.

Brody stood up, climbed onto the table, and rested his head onto the foam cushion as he lay down.

"Did you go out and get a bunch of piercings in your face since the last time I saw you?" The radiology tech, Griffin, was brusque, but nice, and Brody smiled over his joke.

"Not in my face," he teased. "Thank goodness you're not checking my prostate."

"*Oh ho*! And he comes back with a snappy one!" Griffin's ample stomach jiggled with his laughter. "You grew a sense of humor?"

"I've always had one, actually. It's just been hidden by the 'whatever it is' in my skull."

Griffin smiled a sympathetic smile. "See you in about ten minutes." He turned and closed the door behind him.

Brody closed his eyes, held perfectly still, and waited for it to be over.

****

Jess hadn't been to school since Tuesday. It was pretty easy to convince her dad she was sick. Aside from her boyfriend's hospitalization, the discovery of her mother's murder was disturbing, to say the least.

Jess couldn't stop thinking about the photograph and what it might reveal. She wondered when it had happened and if her dad knew. She wondered if maybe it had happened when she was younger and everyone had just *told* her that her mother had run off to spare her the gory details.

And she wondered who was in the picture with her.

Since her mother was still standing upright, she could only assume the other incomplete pair of legs and disembodied elbow belonged to the one who'd murdered her. So then she fantasized about whom did what where with what weapon and concluded this certainly was a true-to-life version of *Clue*. Jess hoped he'd been caught. She hoped he was in jail. She wanted to curse at him and thank him all at the same time.

Jess picked up the phone and tried to call Brody again.

"Room two-twenty-eight, please."

"I'm sorry, Miss, but you just missed him. He's having a test done."

Another test.

One of the problems with her dad believing she was sick was that he wouldn't allow her to go visit Brody in the hospital. And every time she tried to call, he was either having a test done or he was asleep. She hadn't spoken to him or seen him since Tuesday night and she missed him terribly.

The only thing she could do to occupy her time was to attempt to unveil the murderer in the photo. It was slow going and not many of the pictures she took with her camera came back flawed, almost like it was trying to stop her from knowing the truth. She became more and more frustrated with each passing moment. She was being denied her boyfriend and she was being denied her closure.

After several aggravating days of picture taking, printing, snipping and gluing, she finally dropped it all and walked quietly into the living room where her dad was watching television.

"I'd like to go see Brody today."

He looked at her curiously. "Are you feeling better, J-Bird?"

She pretended to smile, and hoped he didn't notice its artificiality. "Yes, Daddy."

"Are you really sure? Not to be offensive, but you don't look so hot."

"Gee. Thanks."

Mr. Waterford huffed. "Now I *told* you I wasn't trying to be offensive."

Jess rocked back and forth on the balls of her feet. "So, can I?"

Her dad seemed to mull it over. "Do you need me to drive you?" he asked finally.

He was going to let her go. "I can walk." Anything so he wouldn't change his mind.

"What time will you be back?"

"When's dinner?"

He looked at his watch. "Noon."

She had apparently aimed too high. "Three?"

"One."

"Two?"

"One-thirty."

"Bye, Daddy." She kissed the top of his head and left for the hospital.

The one thing Jess knew about Nevada weather was that it could be raining one moment, sunshine in another moment, and a blizzard in the next. And if you didn't like any of that, there was always wind. She wrapped her sweater around her face against the biting cold and trudged onward.

Though she remembered the directions she had been given to room 228, curiosity caused her to detour when she thought she caught a glimpse of George walking by in a white lab coat. She followed him as he turned a corner, but when she rounded the bend, he wasn't there. Distracted from her mission, she returned toward her initial destination. When she reached his room, however, she deflated. He wasn't there. Annoyed and disappointed, she approached the nurses' station. "Um … Where's Brody Campbell?"

The young girl in the red and white striped uniform pulled up a clipboard. Her gum almost came out of her mouth when she said, "Campbell?"

"Yes," Jess reiterated. "Brody Campbell."

"Oh, he's having a test."

Again."Well, how long will he be in this 'test'?"

"Um … I dunno … lemme check."

Jess looked down the hallway just in time to see Brody's irritatingly bubbly and exasperatingly attractive nurse wheel him to his room. "Here you go, Handsome!"

Jess made sure to glower at her upon her exit.

But her insecurities eased as soon as Brody reacted to her presence. He hadn't made it into his bed yet, and when he saw her, he walked straight to her and enveloped her in his arms and held her tighter than she thought possible in his condition. "I've missed you *so* much."

She panted involuntarily. "I've missed you, too." She drew him to her in a passionate kiss that was long overdue. "So, so much," she added when they parted.

Brody's dad cleared his throat to announce his presence.

"Did you know he was here?" Jess whispered.

"No." He smiled and turned to his dad. "When did you get here?"

"About five minutes ago," he answered gruffly. "Shouldn't you be in bed?"

Brody kissed Jess on the tip of her nose, winked at her, and pulled both his IV pole and Jess with him toward the bed. Brody wouldn't let go of her hand. "Where have you been?" he asked her. "Why haven't you called?"

"But … but I *have* called. A billion times." Jess tried to withhold her frustration. "Every time I called I got a nurse on the other end of the line that informed me you were in some type of test or another. And apparently they were all too busy to take a message to let you know I'd been trying to reach you."

"Oh. Sorry." Brody pulled her forward and made her sit on the bed next to him. "I wasn't trying to accuse you of anything. I just missed you so much. But none of that matters anymore since you're here now."

Jess smiled halfheartedly. Now that she was here with Brody she wanted to go home and work on her picture and she hated herself for it. She also knew she couldn't say anything about it in front of his dad. She wanted to tell Brody what she'd found, and she wanted to tell him what she was trying to find. She could hardly concentrate on anything else while she knew she had a murder to solve.

"… And go back to school. Jess?"

She hadn't even realized he was talking. "Sorry. I'm just a little distracted, I guess."

"What's wrong?"

She looked at him, scrunched up her face, and then subtly gestured toward his dad. Brody nodded with a knowing look. Jess figured Brody's dad wasn't leaving in the near future, and she was certainly not going to do or say anything in front of him. It made for a dull visit.

"How long do you get to stay?" he asked.

Jess looked at her watch. "Ten." She'd never lied to Brody before and she was amazed at how easily it slipped off her tongue. "I haven't been to school since Tuesday and my dad didn't want me to stay too long."

Brody looked concerned. "Are you sick?"

Jess twirled her hair.

"Oh."

She realized this conversation was just way too difficult with his dad in the room. "I should go." She stood up, but Brody wouldn't let go of her hand.

"But you just got here."

"I'll try to come back later." Was that another lie? She wasn't really sure.

Brody turned toward his dad. "Can you please give me five minutes alone with my girlfriend?"

Mr. Campbell looked a bit put out, but left the room anyway.

"Something is wrong with you, Jess Waterford, and I want to know what it is."

Even though no one else remained in the room to overhear, she leaned in and whispered anyway. "My mom was murdered, Brody. Someone murdered her and whoever did it is in that picture with her."

He appeared to recoil. "How ... how do you know?"

Jess proceeded to tell him about what she'd discovered and what she'd deduced from it.

"But that doesn't mean anything, does it?" Brody fidgeted uneasily. "I think you just need to stop now. You need to throw that picture in the trash or cut it to pieces or burn it to ashes. It's bad, Jess."

Jess looked at her boyfriend like she was seeing him for the first time. "What are you talking about? I need to find out who killed my mother!"

"No, Jess, you don't. That woman was evil to you. She was a raging alcoholic who was abusive both physically and emotionally. She beat your body and she hammered your spirit. You rejoiced when she took off, Jess." He squeezed her hand. "You were happy. You *are* happy. Let it go."

Brody did have a point. She had hated her mother for what she'd done to her. She did exult in her departure. "But I still have to know."

He shook his head in disbelief. "But why?"

She couldn't tell Brody why because she wasn't exactly sure why herself. It was just something that burned within her – almost like desire. And all this arguing over it was eating away valuable time—time that she could be using to finish her photograph. Brody's dad entered the room ending the conversation. "I have to go."

"Please. Just stay a little while longer."

****

Before Jess had time to make up another excuse, four doctors crossed the threshold. Their faces were all expressionless, leaving Brody to believe they weren't exactly there with good news. He'd seen three of them before in one capacity or another, though he hadn't taken the time to learn their names, and none of them had been any good with information spillage since the balding one had told his dad about the "whatever it is."

He figured that was about to change.

And it was Doctor Bald-Guy who spoke first.

"Mr. Campbell, I'm going to try to be as blunt as possible about your son's condition, and you're probably not going to like what we have to say, but we still don't know what's going on with him."

Mr. Campbell stayed silent. Brody assumed his dad didn't like to be put in his place as he had the first time, and he certainly wasn't going to put himself in the position to let it happen again.

"Other than what's going on inside his head, he is healthy in every way. Incredibly 'as a horse' healthy." He looked down at his clipboard. "Every test turned up normal. His blood work was fantastic. His heart is in excellent condition …"

"And I'm handsome, too."

Brody's attempt to lighten the mood fell on deaf ears and Doctor Bald-Guy continued without missing a beat. "But from what we can tell about his head—it's just all been very bizarre. I understand we've been tight-lipped over our findings, sir, but we've all collaborated on this one, and we've even sought expert advice outside our realm. We've been emailing and faxing and comparing and contrasting. We've even flown other doctors in to help." He motioned to the slender Indian doctor to his left. "This is Doctor Bhasin, chief of Neurosurgery at Johns Hopkins."

Dr. Bhasin stepped forward and shook Mr. Campbell's hand.

Doctor Bald-Guy spoke again. "None of us have ever seen anything like this, Mr. Campbell. Nothing even comes close. We've seen solid growths miraculously disappear in one day. We've seen tumors grow from the size of a pea to the size of a baseball in a weekend. We've seen hemorrhages and aneurisms kill people instantly and we've seen others survive them unscathed, and we can't really explain it, but at least we've seen it.

This is very unlike your son's anomaly. His is unique in that sometimes it appears to be liquid and at other times it appears solid. And it's never the same size twice."

"So, it's growing?" His dad could barely squeak out the words.

"And shrinking and growing again."

"Pardon?"

"Exactly."

The chubby but jovial doctor to Bald-Guy's right stood forward. "That's why we had ordered a CT scan every hour on the hour. Your son's mass seems its smallest and more fluid around eight in the evening, and it grows continuously in size and solidity until it reaches its largest volume at approximately two in the morning. It then begins to shrink again, and is at its smallest by eight in the morning, which explains why he is not exhibiting much pain right now at seven-thirty. And the course repeats itself again. However, we have noticed that the mass does get fractionally larger with each cycle."

"So, what does that mean for my son?"

"Well, part of that is up to you." Dr. Bhasin spoke for the first time. His accent wasn't as thick as Brody had expected. "We would like to continue to monitor his progress here, of course. But we do understand it is hard to contain a teenage boy for too long. So we have concluded, provided you are willing, that we will send him home tomorrow morning after an eight o'clock CT scan. We will provide medications that will help him with his pain—and please remember that he will need to be heavily medicated prior to the times when the mass is largest and most concrete. You will need to bring him in at two o'clock the following afternoon, and again at eight o'clock the subsequent morning. This way we may see the progress of the mass when it is at its most extreme state on both sides of the spectrum."

Brody's dad looked at him. "Well, son?"

"I don't think it's up to me, really, Dad. I want to go home. But you're the one who would have to bring me here every day and give me my make-the-pain-go-away happy juice and deal with my screaming and throwing up and nosebleeds. Can you handle all that? And can you miss that much work?"

"Son, I handled all that with your mother. I'm certain I can handle it again. And I haven't taken a vacation or a sick day in seven years. I have over six months of time on the books, and if I need to take them, by God, I'll take them."

"We'll prepare the release paperwork." Dr. Bhasin said, and they all left the room.

Brody's dad put his hand on his son's back. "I'd better go home, too. I have some preparations to make in order to accommodate you at home." He began to exit.

"Dad?"

Mr. Campbell turned around.

"Thank you."

He smiled and left.

Jess just held his hand. She looked numb.

Brody lay back on his pillow and a wave of realization washed over him. It was going to get worse. Unless they could figure out how to stop it, it was growing. Fractionally or not, eventually it was going to eat his brain and kill him.

Chapter Fifteen

"I got called in for a power outage up in Sommerset. Looks like a blown transformer, so you're on your own probably until morning. Have you finished packing?"

Jess looked up from her project and stared blankly at her father. "Just about." She was lying through her teeth, of course, as she'd barely packed a pair of underwear, but she was preoccupied with her quest.

"You leave tomorrow, you know."

Jess scrunched up her face. Tomorrow? Had time passed that quickly? And she *still* hadn't solved her puzzle. She *still* hadn't found her mother's murderer. And she was *so* close. "Okay, Daddy." Her movements mechanical, she set down the photo, several of her fingers bandaged due to the paper cuts and scissor snips of days and days of working, and headed up to her room to pack.

She paid little attention to what she threw haphazardly into her suitcase: bras and underwear, pants, shorts and socks, makeup and shampoo. She wished she could pack her printer. She felt fairly sure only one piece remained of her photograph, and that was more than likely the face of her mother's killer. From what she deduced, the light from the streetlamp illuminated him only partially, and most of his body was cast in dark shadow. But she figured by the angle of his body the light most certainly spilled across his face.

But no matter what she did, that piece wouldn't print. And she was out of photo paper again. She'd been poring over every picture she'd printed in the past just begging for the piece to be there. Praying it was in a picture she'd missed.

She'd even gone so far as to cut the empty centimeter-sized fragment out of the puzzle with an X-acto Knife and place it over each and every photograph a dozen times hoping someone's face would take the place of the missing piece. But nothing fit.

Jess barely thought of Brody, and when her mind did turn to him, she was remorseful over their time apart. When she did have a chance to see him, it was after school at 2:30 in the afternoon and he was comatose on morphine anyway, and when she knew he'd be okay at around 8:00 she was already buried in her murder mystery and was too involved to break away.

But now she was packing and not working on her project and she could think of nothing else *but* Brody.

She looked at the clock—7:45.

Her dad was going to be gone until morning.

She could go, right? She could take the bus, go see him for an hour, and be home by nine-thirty with plenty of time to finish packing for her trip.

Before she was able to contemplate more, the doorbell rang and she flitted down the stairs and yanked open the door. Brody stood there, pale but perfect, and Jess's heart, clearly eight sizes larger than it should have been, thudded in her chest.

"Hi, beautiful." He grinned sideways and leaned casually against the jamb.

The sight of him washed over her in a wave of guilt and she wondered how that lousy picture could have kept her away from him, how she could have neglected him while he was so sick, and how she could have ignored him when she should have been by his side every waking moment.

She stood aside to let him enter, and as soon as he crossed the threshold he closed the door, not taking his eyes off her. He gently set his hands on her hips and snaked them around her waist until he reached her lower back and pulled her into his kiss.

Jess closed her eyes and she felt Brody's chest rise and fall against her as he breathed, his heart thump-thumping audibly. She felt his lips, soft but strong against hers, and his tongue dancing in time with her own. Jess wrapped her arms around his neck and stood on the tips of her toes. His arms tightened around her.

Until that moment, Jess hadn't realized how much she'd missed Brody and how much she had wanted him to be well so he could be with her. She hadn't realized how much time she'd devoted to her photograph and how much time she'd spent away from him. She hadn't realized her yearning for him.

And this time—when Brody's hands wandered—she didn't resist.

****

Brody's eyes fluttered open and the pain in his left temple greeted him like an old foe announcing its plan to fuck up his day.

There was a notable difference this time, and he looked at Jess lying in the bed beside him. He nuzzled closer into her pressing his chest against her back, bare skin on bare skin. He breathed in the soft scent of shampoo in her hair and pressed his lips against her neck, causing her to stir. She rolled over to face him and a smile touched the corners of her eyes.

"I have to finish packing."

She was leaving in a matter of hours. That was why he'd made it a point to go see her in the first place. He'd debated over it every hour he was awake and dreamed of her every hour he wasn't. He didn't know her reasons behind not coming to see him. He figured mostly that she just didn't want to see him in so much pain, so he was bound and determined to not even flinch, even though the ache was growing steadily. As soon as he had seen her he knew he'd made the right decision. And what followed … well, that just confirmed his theory.

"I don't want you to get up. It's been so nice to hold you again. To kiss you again. To … do what we did. Can we do that again?" The throbbing in his temple continued to amplify but he pushed it aside.

"Later, Romeo. If I'm not packed by the time my dad gets home I'm screwed – and not in a good way." She threw the covers off and dressed in the pajamas that had previously been discarded on the floor.

He watched her dart about the room throwing things into her suitcase. "I should probably get something to keep me occupied while I'm on the plane." She exited the room and he heard her feet dance down the stairs.

Brody's head screamed and it was becoming harder and harder to drive it away. He didn't want this to ruin his time with her, but he was unsure how long he could keep it at bay. Beads of sweat formed on his forehead. He quickly wiped them with the sheet on Jess's bed as he heard her feet ascending the stairs.

"I figured I could work on my picture while I'm …" Jess stopped cold when she saw her boyfriend. "Are you okay? Oh, shit, Brody. You don't have your medicine with you and it's almost two!" She dropped the immense pile of photographs and they skittered across her floor. She snatched a tank top out of her dresser drawer and used it to soak up the blood that was trickling down his face.

He hadn't even realized he'd been bleeding. "I'm okay." He took the shirt from her and pinched the bridge of his nose. The pain thundered in his ears.

"Don't lie to me, Brody Campbell. I'm not buying it. As soon as I'm done packing the rest of this, I'm taking you home." She crouched onto her hands and knees and began to pick up the photographs.

"You don't know how to drive," he protested.

Jess froze solid. She stared at the floor, a stack of photos in each hand.

"Jess?"

He watched as a tear fell down her cheek.

"Jess, what are you looking at? What's wrong?"

Pain split Brody's head wide open.

****

Jess barely heard Brody's scream. Tears streamed her cheeks as she looked down at the mess of images on the floor. Her pieced-together photograph landed in her duffel bag, perfectly encircling the photo beneath it. The puzzle was solved, and the murderer was revealed.

It had landed on her passport.

And her own face filled the void.

KIM HARNES

Chapter Sixteen

"Jessica?"

Jess could tell the room was bright on the other side of her eyelids, though she didn't open them for fear of what she might see.

"Jessica, can you hear me?"

She had no idea where she was, who was talking to her, and why on earth her full name was being used. "Jess," she whispered. "Just Jess. And yes, I can hear you."

"She's waking up!" The voice tittered with excitement. "Someone go get the doctor!"

Jess stirred and prepared herself for the glare as she slowly opened her eyes. Not only was the room bright, the walls glowed white, as did the clothes of the three young women within it.

She looked down at her own white attire and gasped—not for what she wore, but what she was beneath. Or, actually, what she wasn't. Her body was emaciated, her skin pallid.

"What's … what's happened to me?" And whose voice was coming out of her? It certainly wasn't *her* voice. Fear swirled through her like a tornado and she sobbed uncontrollably. "Please," she said between her tears. "Please. I'm scared." She pulled her knees into her chest and wrapped her thin arms around her thinner legs.

The three girls in her room looked at her pitifully, apparently not knowing what to do for her. Jess closed her eyes, pressed her forehead against her bony knees and wept. Where was she? And how long had she been there? And where was her father and was Brody okay? And worst of all, had she really been the one to kill her mother? And that picture—*that* picture of her that took the place of the killer's face. The one on her passport. Taken when she was nine years old. Had she really done it that long ago? If she'd really done it, why hadn't anyone told her? Why had they told her that her mother had just left?

The door opened with a series of clicks and clacks. "So, our patient is awake, is she?"

The familiar voice pulled her out of her reverie and she turned toward it in astonishment. "George?"

He smiled wide. His white eyebrows matched his coat and they comically rose into his crinkled forehead as he sat on the bed beside her. "Yes, it's me, Jess." He chuckled warmly. "But I haven't heard you call me George in a long, long time. It's good to hear your voice again."

"It's different." Jess rubbed her throat. "Why is my voice different? And why am I so skinny? And how long is a long time? I just talked to you a couple days ago."

"Easy, Jess." He patted her bony knee. "We've got plenty of time to discuss all of this."

"Doctor Caldwell, do you want me to keep her at her regular dosage?" One of the girls with a clipboard approached George.

"Yes, for the time being," he replied.

What? Jess jumped out of bed and ran to the other side of the room. She pressed her back to the wall, panting doglike in disbelief. "*Doctor* Caldwell? What the hell is going *on?* He's not a doctor!" Jess could feel the anger rising within her, fast and furious. "Who is jerking me around? Joke's over! Where's my dad? And where's Brody?"

George pulled something out of his pocket and he was next to Jess in the blink of an eye. She only realized a syringe pierced her skin after its liquid had already been injected into her arm.

"What are you doing to me?" She tried to pull away, but George had her in a grip stronger than she thought possible of the old man.

"Kathy…some assistance, please?" George remained calm.

The girl with the clipboard approached them and took her other arm. Jess tried again to resist, but her movements became sluggish. Fear replaced anger. She didn't want them to lead her back to the bed, but she was powerless in her defiance. Her eyelids became heavy and were closed before she even felt her head hit the pillow.

****

Jess looked at her mother, repulsed as she paraded around the kitchen, braless in her skimpy tank top and thong underwear. A cigarette dangled between her lips, a whisky-spiked cup of coffee in her hand. "Your dad will be home soon, so get up to your room and do your homework."

"I already did my homework."

She braced herself for the slap she knew would come, and wondered if maybe she even asked for it sometimes—pushed her mother to the brink on purpose.

"I don't give a rat's ass if you have homework or not. You will be upstairs when your dad gets home."

The fire on her cheek where she'd been hit was nothing compared to the white-hot anger within her. "Maybe you can have sex with Daddy and get pregnant again so you'll have someone else to blame for your body besides me."

But her mother was ready with her retaliation. She took Jess by both hands and slammed her against the refrigerator, causing the freezer to open above her and spill its contents on her head. "Maybe I can. And maybe if I do, she won't be an unappreciative little whore who doesn't know just how good she's got it." *The cigarette, still clenched in her mother's teeth, pressed into the left side of Jess's forehead searing her flesh. She tried to pull away from her mother's grip, but she couldn't move.*

Jess screamed and tried again to tug free, but the bindings on her wrists held firm. She kicked and thrashed and screamed at the dark, completely disoriented in her surroundings and scared to death.

She was afraid to open her eyes for fear of what she would see—hoping she would be in her own bedroom, but sure she would be in hell with the rotting corpse of her mother. She screamed and fought, screamed and fought, until there was no fight left in her and she slowly sank into the darkness.

"That ought to hold her 'til morning," George said, and *her mother cackled through her yellow teeth. "Hold her 'til morning. Good."*

****

Jess wasn't sure how long she teetered on the edge of fantasy and reality, nor could she tell the difference between the two.

Occasionally she would open her eyes to see George, smiling his wrinkle-faced smile. Mostly he was wearing his white smock, but at times he wore jeans and a collared shirt.

Once in awhile she'd see her dad. Seldom did he look as she thought he should look, and frequently he looked older. Haggard. Sad.

Thankfully, less and less often she saw her mother. It was these images that scared her most because she never knew if she would look as she remembered her—inadequately clothed and enveloped in a nicotine mist, or if she would be covered in blood—expressionless as she was in her picture, or if she would be even worse—decayed and gruesome, covered in rot and stink. She was frightening in all three forms, and always reached out for her as if to pull her with her into the murk she'd come from and release her vengeance. *"Come with me, Jessica,"* she'd say as she beckoned her. *"I know you'll like it here."* Shivering, she would bury her face into her pillow and hope it all went away.

She even saw Carter Benson a time or two—always in that blue shirt that now, every once in awhile, looked like hospital apparel.

But she never saw Brody.

Her mind made up thousands of reasons as to why he hadn't come to see her, and none of them were good. He didn't love her anymore. His dad found out what they'd done and refused to let him see her. He'd gotten what he wanted and now he was done with her. His head exploded and he was dead.

She tried to talk to everyone she saw in an attempt to get some answers. No one would tell her anything, and that was beginning to piss her off. George kept telling her there was plenty of time, and they would work it all out, and my, wasn't she progressing well, and a bunch of other bullshit that wasn't answering her questions.

From what she could tell she slept a lot, mostly due to heavy sedatives. They seemed to be wearing off, however, and it appeared her "awake times" were growing longer and longer. She even began to gain a little weight.

Finally, after what seemed like months, George entered her room, pulled over a chair, and sat down by her bed. He looked at her curiously, rubbed the scruffy white whiskers on his chin, and before Jess could belt out her usual barrage of questions, he spoke.

"I think … yes. I think it's time."

Chapter Seventeen

George stood and left the room leaving Jess to gawk after him in bewilderment. Time? *Time for what?* Time to give her answers? Time to let her go home? Time to let her see Brody?

Seventy-eight seconds of eternity later and a large and familiar looking nurse walked in with fresh pajamas to replace her white cotton gown. Jess knew she'd seen her before, but she couldn't quite put a finger on it. It didn't really matter where she thought she might have known her from—she was a hospital employee who most likely had answers.

"What's going on? Where's George? What is he doing? Am I going home? Where's Brody?" Her excitement grew over the anticipation of some response and each question gained emphasis until she was almost screaming.

But the nurse just smiled and left Jess alone with her pajamas.

"Where are you going? Come back and talk to me!"

The lock clicked.

With nothing else to do and no one else to yell at, she changed her clothes, put on her slippers, and walked around the room. Her eyes were gradually growing accustomed to the whiteness of it.

After about a half hour of mindless wandering, the door finally opened behind her and the nurse who had brought her clothes appeared with a wheelchair. "Ready?"

"Ready for what?"

"I'm taking you to Doctor Caldwell's office. He wants to talk to you."

Talk. To *Doctor* Caldwell. She had met nothing but adversity trying to explain he was a photographer and not a doctor, so she'd stopped trying to convince anyone and figured she had probably just better play along. "Is he going to answer my questions, or is he just going to ask me a bunch more?"

The nurse smiled again. "I think it's going to be a two-sided conversation."

Good enough. Jess took her seat in the chair and let the nurse lead her onward. The halls were as white as her room and she passed several doors with small windows like hers. It was noisier as well, like the halls of her high school between periods. The patients and orderlies, doctors and nurses skittered in and out of rooms in the hospital just as the students and teachers did on their way to class when the bell rang.

After two lefts and a right Jess finally realized where she thought she'd seen the nurse before and she looked up at her. "Do you have a sister?"

"Why, yes I do."

"Does she drive a Citifare bus?"

She smiled warmly. "No. My sister lives in Seattle and doesn't get down here much."

"Oh." So she was wrong. But the resemblance was uncanny. "Well, you have someone who looks just like you who drives a bus."

Two more turns and they were outside an office with a large placard that read, "Dr. George Caldwell, M.D., Psy.D. LCPC." Jess flinched at the sign, for it seemed to be solid proof George was indeed a doctor. This, of course, prompted her with a half billion more questions she was prepared to ask him when she had the chance, though she also mostly feared the reply. The nurse balled her plump fist and rapped on the door.

"Enter." George's muffled voice came from the other side.

The nurse put the brakes on the chair and opened the door. "You can go in."

Jess rose timidly and entered George's office. The carpet was thick and fluffy and the furniture was cozy, and not as rigid as she'd anticipated. Beautiful framed photographs covered almost every inch of all four walls, with the exception of one area, which held his multiple degrees and certifications.

"Have a seat, Jessica."

"Jess." She always preferred her nickname, but it sounded foreign to her when it rolled off her own tongue with someone else's voice.

George smiled. "I'd forgotten. I'm sorry, Jess. Please sit down."

Jess sat stiffly and wrapped her arms around her middle.

"Are you cold? Do you need a robe or a blanket?"

Prickly goose bumps rippled her gaunt flesh and she nodded eagerly. George pressed the intercom on his desk and summoned a nurse for the items. She appeared immediately and wrapped Jess in white terrycloth warmth.

"Now," George said and clasped his hands together. "I want to lay some ground rules before we get started."

Jess blinked. "Ground rules?"

"Yes. I have rules you will need to follow, or our session will end."

"Our session?" Jess went from believing she was sick to understanding she was crazy. "Holy shit, George."

George smiled at her the way he always had when she'd cursed in his presence. He pulled out a recorder, a notebook, and a pen from his drawer and set them on his desk next to a thick file.

"I will be asking you a lot of questions, of which I expect you to answer to the best of your knowledge. In return, I will attempt to answer some of the questions you have as well. Bear in mind, though, I will not reveal what I deem to be too much information to you all at once, as I believe it would be detrimental to your recovery. Do you understand?"

Jess nodded. Fear filled her core and anger shot out from her extremities.

George must have seen the flicker of ire within her. "Also, you've seen how quickly I can get someone into this room with a robe and blanket. Rest assured I can get someone in here just as quickly with a straitjacket and a vial of Thorazine."

Jess looked at her skeletal fingers entwined in her lap, and nodded again.

"Very well. We will start off by my letting you ask one question. Please take your time and choose this question carefully. This should be the one question you want answered most."

Jess mentally rifled through vast amount of questions that were swimming in her mind and her eyes fell upon Brody's leather bracelet encircling her wrist. *Where was he?* That was certainly the first question she had. But was it most important? Had she really killed her mother? She assumed she already knew the answer to that question, considering her current location. Finally she took another look at her wasted frame and made her decision.

"How long have I been here?"

George leaned back in his chair. Jess assumed he was debating on whether or not it was a question he would answer. But to her surprise he sat up. "Seven years."

Jess's stomach roiled and her heart clobbered her ribcage from the inside. "Seven *years*? How is that possible? I'm twenty-three years old?"

George leaned back in his chair again and pulled the cap off the pen. "How old did you think you were?"

"Sixteen." Jess sniffled.

"What month is it?"

The fear and anger both rose exponentially within her, each trying to overpower the other. So far, fear was winning. "I … I don't know now, I guess. I thought it was May."

George wrote something down on his notepad. "And how long did you think you'd been in here?"

Jess wondered about how much time had passed since she'd figured out her picture and how many days she had bordered on the realm of unconsciousness since. "A couple weeks, maybe."

"And what do you think now?" George hadn't looked up from his notepad and was still scribbling frantically.

"I guess there's no way possible for me to have lost this much weight in a couple weeks."

George finally looked at her. "Excellent and lucid deduction."

Jess smiled at George's compliment. She'd always loved it when he'd praised her work in the past. "Do I get any more questions?"

"Not just yet. I want to know more about you first."

Anger took the lead in her battle of emotions. "But I want to know more about me, too! Damn it, George, what the hell is going on here?"

"You need to calm down, Jess."

She stood on her stick legs and leaned over the desk as menacingly as her small body would allow. "Don't tell me to calm down! I need to know, George!"

"This is your last warning, Jess. Sit down now or we're done for today."

Jess saw George's left hand shift toward the button on his desk and she stopped. The anger still coursed through her and she gripped the edge of the desk until her fingers ached and she was sure she must have been breathing fire. She was angry, yes. But she was still in control of her faculties for the time being. She knew she still had questions and didn't want to ruin her chances to get them answered. She slowly backed away. "What else do you want to know?" It was difficult to speak with her jaw locked.

George looked at her as though he were sizing her up. "Maybe we should be done for the day, Jess. I don't want to pressure you with too much too soon."

"NO!"

George remained calm. "You are not well, Jess, nor will you get well if you continue this way. I just want to help you. And I can't help you if we can't talk."

Jess continued to speak through clenched teeth. "So answer my questions and we'll talk."

"All in good time. Now, may I continue?"

"Go for it." Rage bubbled at the surface of her skin raising her body temperature and making her sweat. She removed the robe and blanket, discarded them on the floor, and sat back down.

"Jess, do you know why you're here?"

Her eyes were slits. "I assume it's because I killed my mother."

George cleared his throat. "Do you remember how it happened?"

"No."

"No, you don't remember? Or no, you don't want to tell me?"

Bastard. "No, I don't remember. Do *you* want to tell me?"

"Not yet, no."

She figured as much. Her skin sizzled.

"How about *why* it happened, Jess? Do you remember that?"

Jess's body became rigid. "I remember she was an alcoholic bitch who thought it was fun and games to slap me around."

"Slap you around?" George wrote on his notepad again. "When did she do this?"

The fury within her progressed from bubble to full boil. "Constantly."

He looked back through several pages of her chart. "There is nothing in here that suggests your mother beat you, Jessica."

"CALL ME JESS, DAMN IT!"

Jess's world turned black.

****

Jess awoke to pain.

Her entire body ached—every joint, every muscle. And she was tied up again, both wrists *and* ankles this time. Minimal light came through the small window in her door, not nearly bright enough to see what it was that crusted her pajamas to her right side. She smelled like body odor and urine.

Struggling was superfluous, and since she couldn't move, she tried to glean what she could from the only question answered in her meeting with George. She'd been here seven years. Seven. She'd missed her twenty-first birthday. She'd missed her father's fiftieth. That certainly explained why he'd looked so haggard in the few flashes she'd seen of him.

She'd also missed out on seven years with Brody, which explained why he hadn't come to see her. She wondered how his bracelet had ended up on her wrist. If the "whatever it was" in his skull hadn't killed him first, he'd probably have already moved on. Found another girlfriend, or possibly a wife. Forgotten all about her.

The thought of Brody holding someone else was more than she could bear and the pain in her muscles was nothing compared to the agony in her heart.

She sobbed in the dark alone and pitiful, unable to stop the tears from coming, and without the means to wipe them away.

Jess thought she heard movement outside her door and called out. "Is anybody there?" She pulled against her restraints, but every movement screamed at her in protest. "Hello? Can anyone hear me?"

She wasn't sure anyone wanted to.

But almost instantly her door opened and two people entered, barely visible in the dark. Jess could only tell one was large and one wasn't, and they were both coming at her, neither of them friendly. She struggled to get away, but pain racked her withered muscles. The larger one held her still. The smaller one stuck a needle in her.

"Wait, no, please! I'm fine! Don't do this to me! What is happening to me?"

STILL PHOTO

And for the second time that day her world went black.

KIM HARNES

Chapter Eighteen

This time when Jess's eyes opened the room was bright and she wasn't alone. George was sitting in a chair by her bed, a bandage over his left eye and another on his left hand.

"Holy crap, George." Jess was able to sit up, but as soon as she did, two people she hadn't seen grabbed her from each side and wrapped her tightly in a white jacket. "What the … let me out of this thing!"

They didn't listen, of course, and as soon as they were certain she was immobile, they left the room.

"Why?" Jess cried.

"It's for your protection as much as it is for mine." George had the notebook in his lap, his pen held gingerly in his injured hand.

"What happened?"

"You don't know?" George looked at Jess, but wrote slowly on the tablet.

"Should I know?" How the hell should she know?

"Think about our session, Jess. Can you remember our session?"

"Most of it." She leaned back against her pillow, which the orderlies had propped up behind her. She didn't really remember much of anything except how she felt—like her veins were swirling with evil. "I know I was very angry."

"Yes, you were."

"I don't remember how I got back to my room."

"What was the last thing you do remember, Jess?"

The mention of her name helped her recall the last bit. "You had called me Jessica and that pissed me off. Then I guess I passed out."

153

"Do you want to try to remember the rest?"

She didn't even know there was more to remember and, eying George's present condition, she wasn't exactly sure she wanted to. Yet she hated not knowing. "I … I don't know. I guess so. But how can you make me remember?"

"I'm going to attempt to help you. I need you to lie back and close your eyes." George moved the pillows away and lowered the top of the bed so she could position herself horizontally. "Now I want you to release every other thought from your mind and relax."

Jess fought hard to not think about anything, though mountains of questions and horrific thoughts and feelings of anger and fear pounded in on her making it impossible. "I can't."

"You can, Jess. Listen to my voice. Nothing can harm you right now."

Jess breathed deeply against the jacket that surrounded her torso and listened to George's voice.

"I want you to concentrate on a small white light in a black, black room. Do you see it?"

Jess did as she was told. The small white light presented itself before her, and it was surrounded by darkness. "Yes."

"Good. Now that small white light is growing little by little by little, and your memory is behind that light. Can you see it?"

Jess imagined the light growing bigger. "Yes."

"Good. We're almost there. Now I want you to reach your mind through to the other side of the light and remember. Are you reaching?"

Jess reached.

Her room faded away and *she was back in George's office, both of them in their respectable places on either side of his desk. She felt the anger stirring inside her as he looked through her chart.*

"There is nothing in here that suggests your mother beat you, Jessica."

"CALL ME JESS, DAMN IT!"

Jess leapt and in one swift movement both feet landed solidly on the top of George's desk. Her eyes darted toward his left hand, which was attempting to summon security, and she deftly swiped the pen from his grip and stabbed it hard into the flesh between his index and middle fingers and an inch deep into the desktop pinning him out of reach of the button.

She turned and saw the fear in George's eyes, only inches away from hers. She'd always hated those eyebrows. She bit and George screamed. Blood oozed down her chin as she spit white fur onto the floor and whooped around the room like a warrior who'd just scalped his enemy. Jubilant. Exhilarated.

Nutty as squirrel shit.

Someone grabbed her from behind and she struggled. And she bit. And she kicked and she punched and she clawed. She urinated on herself. Her bare foot hit solidly into someone's groin and she heard him moan deep in his throat. Victory consumed her as his eyes rolled back into his head and his knees hit the fuzzy carpet.

Several people tackled her at once and she was finally subdued, though she still made every attempt to thrash free. Blood mixed with drool dribbled from her maniacal smile.

A needle pierced her skin.

"You fuckers don't fight fair."

The rebellion within her surrendered as the fluid sped through her veins.

"Jess?"

"George?"

"It's time to come back to this side of the light now."

Jess obeyed. The light became smaller and smaller. Her cheeks were wet and her body that once hurt with strain now ached with remorse. "Oh, God, George. I'm so sorry. I'm so sorry I did that to you."

His pen scratched slowly along the notepad. "I believe you. And I accept your apology. But let's just say until I'm sure it won't happen again, we'll have our sessions under the present conditions. Agreed?"

She looked once again at her bondage. Did she agree? After that episode, she didn't exactly blame him. But did she like it? Not really, no, but she didn't really have a choice. She nodded somberly.

"Good. Now, I'm very excited we were able to retrieve that memory from you, and I think I'm going to use that technique several more times during your treatment – to help you remember, and help me understand."

Jess just stared blankly at George. She wasn't sure if she liked that, either.

"I hate that I have to be restrictive on my information to you, but you have to understand that too much all at once can send you spiraling into another violent attack. That not only endangers you and those around you, but you take steps backward in your therapy. I don't want either of those things."

"Can … can I still ask questions?"

George wrinkled his forehead, and then apparently immediately regretted his mistake as fresh blood dampened his bandaged brow. "You may, but I won't guarantee I'll answer them. And, unfortunately, that is another trigger for your anger. I would recommend you keep your queries to a minimum."

Jess nodded.

"But you may ask one now."

Jess felt sadness sting the backs of her eyes. She no longer cared about herself or her recovery and she loathed what she had done to George. Her thoughts rested upon the bracelet around her wrist and she felt the braided leather rope press against her skin within her constraints. "Is Brody happy?" The tears fell as she braced herself for his response.

"Brody. Ah, yes, Brody." George was silent for a long while. He rubbed the coarse whiskers on his chin, visibly contemplating his reply. "I don't know how to answer that one, Jess. Not right now."

"Okay." She didn't want that to be the answer. She wanted to know about where he was and who he was with, regardless of whether she was out of the picture. She wanted to know if he were playing baseball and with what team and was he in the Major Leagues yet. She wanted to know if he were still alive. But the answers weren't going to be given.

"There is one thing I believe I can tell you, though." George seemed to mull the words over in his mind as if trying to find a way to say what he had to say that would upset her least.

Jess's breathing and heartbeat accelerated in anticipation of some shred of enlightening information. The straitjacket constricted her chest with each lungful of air.

"Your dad misses you."

"My ... my dad?" Not that she wasn't touched by the gesture, but it was news about her dad. Not news about Brody.

"Yes. He's been here quite a bit to see you the past seven years. If you can behave and if he can promise not to say anything … damaging to you, I've arranged a visit for this evening."

Knowing she wasn't getting any more information about Brody at this particular moment in time, Jess thought she would probably like a visit from her dad. She couldn't possibly miss him as much as he missed her, though, considering he hadn't seen her in seven years and she just saw him a couple weeks ago—in her timeframe, anyway. "I can behave," she said timidly.

"Do you promise?"

Jess smiled at George. "Yes, I promise." And she giggled to herself a little when she realized her arms were crossed in front of her in her straitjacket. Promises didn't count when something was crossed, did they?

"Good. Now today I want you to tell me about what led you to me."

Jess didn't understand what he meant.

He apparently read the confusion in Jess's face. "I want you to tell me everything you know. Everything about your life as far back as you can remember."

"That's a pretty long story, isn't it?"

George flexed his wounded hand. "I've got the time. How about you?"

Jess had to laugh. It wasn't as if she had a hot date. "I guess so."

"As far back as you can remember."

George readied his pen and Jess began her tale.

After two hours of talking, Jess had only reached the age of six. George appeared to listen to every word with tremendous interest. She mentioned how her mother pranced around the house half naked. She mentioned the alcohol abuse. She mentioned the plastic camera incident and dozens more like it.

Jess watched George intensely, but his actions were hard to read. He would frown and write and smile and write and chuckle and write. She only felt pangs of anger when she spoke of her mother's abuse. Speaking of it, in a way, made her feel the hurt all over again, as if she were reliving the memory. But she was so glad to get it all off her chest, and all in all, she kept her cool. And George was appreciative.

"Excellent work today, Jess. Just excellent."

Jess beamed at the accolade as George stood to leave.

"I do believe it's lunchtime. What do you say to some food?"

Jess looked down at her body still tethered in her jacket. "I'd say who's gonna feed me?"

George chuckled. "We'll get that off you."

"Can I have it off for our next session, too?" Jess batted her eyelashes innocently.

George motioned to his missing eyebrow with his damaged hand. "You may have to give me a few more sessions before I'm ready to trust that again."

Jess was swift to quash the anger this time and she nodded in agreement.

Almost immediately after George's departure, the same people who had strapped her into her jacket removed her from it and exited silently.

Despite her sore muscles Jess stretched her body as far as it would go, glad to be free of her restraints. Minutes later a man walked in with a tray of food. He was dressed in a blue shirt and pants and Jess thought he looked amazingly like someone she knew. When he moved a table to her and set her food down on it Jess sucked in her breath as realization hit her.

"Carter?" She stared at him in disbelief. "Carter Benson?"

Chapter Nineteen

Carter stood up straight and looked at her curiously.

"It's me, Carter. Jess Waterford."

"I know who you are, Jess. I'm just surprised you remember *me*." He opened a package and unfolded a small moist towel. "Here, let me get this for you." He began to wipe her chin, and she figured there was probably still a fair amount of blood and spit left over from her rampage. Then she was embarrassed over her own foul scent of urine and body odor and hoped he didn't notice.

"Of course I remember you." She continued to talk as he cleaned her up. Really, how could she not remember Carter? He was friends and teammates with her boyfriend. And he had answers. She went for broke. "Do you keep in touch with Brody? Is he okay? Is he playing baseball?"

Carter frowned and threw the towel away. "I'm … I'm really not supposed to talk to you about anything, Jess. Sorry. Dr. Caldwell's orders."

Jess's balloon of hope deflated. "Okay. I understand."

He touched her knee and smiled. "It's good to see you awake."

"Nice to see you're still a 'chick magnet' in your blue shirt. It really does bring out your eyes."

Carter grinned, blushed, and shook his head. "You amaze me, Jess Waterford. That's for sure." He exited the room and locked it behind him.

Despite her current circumstances, she smiled for the rest of the day over seeing Carter – some piece of her past that wasn't tarnished with secrets and murder and hand stabbing and eyebrow biting. He couldn't talk to her yet, but eventually, if she behaved, she was sure to have many conversations with him about high school and Brody and baseball and good times.

After she'd eaten she was allowed to shower so she'd be clean when her dad arrived. She finally noticed the blood on her pajamas—the reason they were caked to her skin. George's blood.

The nurse allowed her entrance to the large bathroom and handed her a towel and a bag of toiletries, which she set on the counter and removed one by one: a bar of soap, a small wash cloth, a bottle of shampoo, a comb, a toothbrush, and a small tube of toothpaste. There'll be no razor for *this* psycho, she thought to herself.

Even though she wanted to shower desperately, her mouth tasted of bile and blood and her tongue felt thick with plaque. She opted to take care of that first. She screwed the cap off the toothpaste, applied it to her toothbrush, and looked in the mirror for the first time.

Her screams bounced off the white tiled walls and amplified with the room's natural acoustics.

It wasn't the Jess Waterford she knew in that mirror.

She looked like her mother. Only more frightening.

She pulled at her hair and brought it in front of her eyes to see if it were actually red and curly as it was in her reflection and not light brown and straight as it was in her memory and that made her scream more.

She touched her face and eyes and ears and hair to make sure her reflection did the same thing and it did, and still she screamed louder.

The last seven years had caused her sallow skin to hang loosely on her scrawny body, and beneath her sunken gray eyes and hollow cheeks dried blood intermingled with toothpaste foam and trailed down her chin and neck like a mad, rabid dog.

And still the screams came.

"Enough of that, or I'll call Security!" the nurse bellowed from the door.

Screams were replaced by sobs. "Why … why do I look this way?"

"Look what way?" The nurse was apparently uninterested.

"Like this. I am Jess Waterford, not Amanda, right? Please tell me I'm Jess Waterford." She had to be Jess. Everyone was calling her Jess.

"Look at your bracelet, idiot."

She looked at the piece of plastic encircling her wrist and closed her eyes. She *was* Jess Waterford. Jess. When she opened her eyes the bracelet would say Jess and she would look normal again.

She dared to take a peek at the bracelet and confirmed with relief that she was, in fact, Jess Waterford. But her reflection was unchanged. She dropped to the hard tile floor and cried.

"You need to knock that crap off and get in the shower like you've been told to do."

Jess's tears were relentless. "I don't understand why I look this way."

"It's called genetics. Now get up."

"Why do I have to look like *her*?"

After the threat of another needle, Jess's sobbing ceased and the nurse pushed her toward the shower so she could scrub off the blood and the urine and the sweat. She tried to scrub the mom off her face, but she was unsuccessful. The hot water beat down on her and she let it soak her hair and her body as she lathered and rinsed. She figured she'd had nothing more than a sponge bath over the last seven years and she reveled in the cleansing she felt—both body and soul. She would've stayed in there for hours if she could have. But the nurse told her it was time to get out, so she turned off the shower and dried off.

She felt better.

She smelled better.

She was led back to her room to wait for her dad. And she waited. And waited. And waited some more.

Finally the would-be twin of her bus driver showed up with two security guards. The guards strapped her (with no resistance) into her straitjacket, and the nurse wheeled her to George's office.

Her dad was there, sitting in the chair she'd been in before she attacked George. He looked nervous.

And old. Really old. Gray and white peppered his dark brown hair and deep worry lines channeled across his brow.

"Hey, J-Bird." He stood to greet her, and he wrapped his arms gingerly around her shoulders.

"I'd hug you back, but …" Jess smiled over her own joke about her current confinement.

Her dad cleared his throat and looked at his feet.

"Why don't you both sit down?" George motioned to the second chair and indicated Jess should occupy it, which she did after guiltily stepping over a blood stain on the carpet from where she'd spit out a chunk of his forehead.

They all sat there in uncomfortable silence for what seemed like days to Jess, each one of them waiting for the other to speak first, and all apparently afraid to say the wrong thing. Finally her dad broke the silence.

"I've missed you, J-Bird."

Safe enough thing to say, Jess thought. It wasn't as if she could really reciprocate the feeling, but she reciprocated the gesture. "I've missed you, too, Daddy."

He smiled as if that were the best thing he'd ever heard, and Jess was instantly glad she'd said it. She wasn't exactly sure what else they'd be able to converse about, considering there was to be no mention of her mother, Brody, or anything else important. And it wasn't as if she were up on current events, or even the weather for that matter. But despite their limited list of topics, they found a few things to discuss.

"So, are you still working for the power company?" Her dad's job was another safe zone.

"I am. And I don't get called out on graveyard shift anymore. I actually got promoted, so I'm the one that gets to do the calling."

"That's great. I know how much you hated that."

"It did keep me away from the house a lot."

Yeah, Jess thought. *And left me home alone with her so she could kick my ass.* She breathed in deeply through her nose and exhaled the resentment.

George scribbled on his notepad.

Jess changed the subject and rattled off several more options. "So, what's going on in the world lately? Have the Giants won a pennant? Did California fall into the ocean yet?"

Wesley chuckled softly. "Reno actually has its own Triple-A baseball stadium right downtown. Maybe if you get better George will let me take you to a game."

Jess looked hopefully at George, who only smiled and continued to scribble on his notepad. Then she

165

looked down at her torso, which was still mummy-like in her restraints. She'd have to get a *lot* better if she were going to get to go out in public.

"The Giants did better than win a pennant," Wesley continued. "A couple years ago, they took the World Series with a rookie catcher."

Jess's ears perked. Brody could have been that rookie catcher. Was he playing with the Giants? George and Wesley both appeared to have read her thoughts almost as clearly as if she'd spoken them out loud.

"California's still where it belongs," he continued, skirting the now taboo subject of baseball.

They continued talking about other useless and unimportant things and George continued to doodle on his tablet. The mood continued to remain as light as was possible for a room containing a man and a doctor and a loon. The thought caused Jess to giggle.

"It's good to see you smile, Jess." Her dad looked at her proudly. "And you're putting on some weight and you have color. I'm glad."

"Thanks, Daddy."

"You're welcome, J-Bird."

Jess grinned shyly and teased her father. "Yeah, well, you're looking pretty old, there, Pop."

The next words came out of his mouth presumably of their own accord as if he'd recited them a hundred times before to anyone who'd made the same comment. "Of course I look old. That's what losing your wife and children all in one day does to a man."

"Children?" Jess was sure she'd heard him correctly. "You said child*ren.* As in more than one."

Wesley looked pleadingly at George who appeared as though he was rapidly thinking of something to say to undo the damage.

But there was no taking that back.

Jess's insides begin to boil and churn, but she held her temper. Getting angry and blowing her top wasn't going to get her anywhere. Neither was jumping on George's desk, gripping his shiny and expensive pen between her toes, and stabbing her dad in the neck with one swift kick. She shook the thought from her brain and internally scolded herself for thinking it in the first place. She stood slowly so as not to alarm either of them. "I don't imagine you're going to answer any questions I may have about a brother or sister I don't know about," she said calmly. "So I'm ready to go back to my room now."

George nodded and summoned the nurse who was there immediately to wheel her away. When she arrived at her room she was released from her restraints and she quietly lay down and pulled her knees into her chest.

Jess didn't understand anything anymore. She didn't understand why she suddenly looked like her mother. She didn't understand how she had a sibling. She didn't understand why no one would tell her about Brody.

And she didn't understand how she'd blacked out in George's office.

Had she done that before, she wondered—blacked out with no memory of it? She certainly didn't remember actually killing her mother, though she knew she had.

Had she killed her brother or sister, too?
Had she killed Brody?

Jess cried into her pillow, her body curled into a ball, her left hand entangled in her hair, the bright white room mocking her murky disposition. She remained that way even after a rough voice that sounded creepily like Brody's dad's militant tone announced 'lights out' and the only beam that remained came through the six-by-ten inch frame of Plexiglas in her door. It illuminated a small square on the white tiled floor.

Jess released every other thought from her mind. She concentrated on the small white light in the black, black room and reached for her memories on the other side.

Chapter Twenty

Jess was way ahead of her dad and she could hear him wheeze loudly behind her as they climbed the side of the hill. "Come on, Daddy! Hurry up!! You're sooooooo slooooowwwwwwww!"

"Hold on J-Bird! You're going too fast for me." He huffed and puffed and finally caught up with her as she reached the pond, their destination atop Peavine.

Jess's heavy and archaic camera hung from her neck. "But I want to get a really good picture, Daddy! George said if I get a really, really good one he'll frame it for his wall!"

"The trees aren't going anywhere, Sweetie." Wesley was hunched over, his hands on his knees, trying to catch his breath.

"But the bird in the tree might go somewhere." She darted around the forest snapping pictures and advancing the film. When she'd used up a roll, she painstakingly rewound it and added more. As she did so, the tip of her tongue protruded from the corner of her mouth and her face was scrunched in deep concentration. After she'd exhausted her supply, she packed up the camera and joined her dad on the blanket where he sat unwrapping sandwiches.

"Get some good ones?" Wesley moved a strand of hair out of her face.

"Hope so." She looked up at her father and felt love in her heart. She really wanted to be part of George's wall. George was her dad's friend and he was a really good listener and he taught her how to focus a camera and take good pictures. She also got to talk to him about all sorts of things. Except her mom. Brody told her she shouldn't talk to him about her mom. He said

169

George wouldn't understand. But she really liked to go see him so she could look at all the pictures all over his walls. Her eyes danced over the framed glory of everything imaginable in every color possible. To get her picture on that wall for other people to see. That would be an honor. Even better than a home run.

"Good sandwich?" Her dad smiled at her as she polished off the last bite.

"Mmm hmm."

"Good. Listen, J-Bird, I know it's been awhile since you and I have come up here, but I really need to talk to you about something serious."

Jess scrunched her nose. Nine-year-old girls didn't like serious.

"I ... well ..." He fidgeted a little and Jess cocked her head. "What would you say to a brother or sister?"

"I'd say, 'Hi, don't steal my toys.'"

Wesley chuckled. "So you'd be okay with the idea?"

Jess thought about it. Yes, she would love another brother or sister to play with. She would love to help take care of him or her. But her mother—what would she do? Jess couldn't help but think her mother would hate the baby, too, the way she hated Jess. She might blame it for ruining her body worse and beat it up, too. And her mom drank a lot of alcohol and she knew you weren't supposed to drink alcohol if you had a baby in your tummy. She figured out the bads outweighed the goods.

"No. I don't think so."

Her dad seemed surprised by her response. "Well, why not?"

Jess thought hard about what she should say. She certainly couldn't tell her dad the real reasons. She'd tell Brody the real reasons later.

"Well, 'cause if you have another baby girl I won't be your Little Princess anymore."

Wesley smiled. "You'll always be my Little Princess."

"Well, I still don't want one."

"What if it's a brother? You could teach him how to play baseball."

Jess began to rip apart a pine cone piece by piece as she thought of her new excuse. "Nah. With you and George and Brody I think I already have enough boys in my life."

That one caused her dad to laugh out loud. "Too much testosterone for you?"

Jess scrunched her nose again. "What's tesposkerone?"

"It's ... something I'll tell you about when you're older."

"I just don't think I'd like sharing my stuff with anybody – boy or girl."

"Well, babies get their own stuff, too."

Jess picked up another pine cone and chucked it across the clearing. "Mom tells me all the time you guys can't even afford me. How are you gonna afford another baby?"

Her dad seemed to shrink. "Your mom said that?"

Jess thought of a hundred bad words in her head but didn't say any of them out loud. Instead, she grabbed another pine cone to quietly disassemble.

After what seemed like hours of silence, Wesley finally perked up. "Hey, look what I found!" He produced a new roll of film from his coat pocket.

Jess smiled hugely at her dad, snatched the film from his hand, and ran off to get the picture that would take a place on George's wall.

****

Jess was surprised George had asked to see her, and even more so when she was allowed to be free of her straitjacket. When she entered his office, however, he wasn't in it. She wandered around the room and looked at the pictures on George's wall until she reached the one she was looking for: an ornately framed photo of a monarch butterfly emerging from its cocoon. She gently caressed the frame with her fingertips.

"You're remembering." George's usually gruff voice was soft behind her.

"I was so proud when you put this picture up here. Like I'd won the World Series, the Super Bowl, and the Stanley Cup all rolled into one."

"It's a beautiful picture."

A tear slid down Jess's cheek. "My mother was pregnant when I killed her."

George's hand was on her shoulder, firm, yet gentle. "Why don't you sit down and we can talk about it."

"We can talk about it?"

George brushed at the tear that now dribbled down her chin and spoke as he sat down at his desk. "You handled yourself very well with your father – with the information he let slip. It was encouraging. And I gained some trust in you."

Jess swung her arms around. "I see that." She reveled in her own freedom.

"So, are you going to sit?"

Jess eyed the chair. She wanted to sit down and have her questions answered. But she was also afraid. She feared she wouldn't like the answers she received, and she feared she would react horribly when that ended up being the case. She stood still.

"Jess?"

She jumped at the sound of his voice, and then slowly made her way to her seat.

"To answer your question: Yes, your mother was pregnant at the time of her demise."

"Demise? Why don't you just say murder, George? Isn't that what it was?" Though she felt a twinge of anger, she remained calm.

George scribbled in his notebook. "Yes. Murder." George cleared his throat. "Now, at our last session we'd gotten right up almost to your seventh birthday. What do you remember after that?"

Jess thought back: Her seventh birthday. What a day to remember. Jess had had no friends to speak of, so there was no fanfare. Her mother had gotten slobbering drunk by two in the afternoon and vomited all over the only present she'd received—a Princess costume. The tag had read, "Love Mom and Dad," but she knew who'd picked it out. Her mom then proceeded to shove her by her face into the pile of sick knocking her tooth loose. She then yelled at her to clean up the mess, and passed out cold on the floor between the couch and the coffee table. Happy birthday.

George continued to write. "And what happened after that?"

Jess smiled. "The next day the tooth went missing. Mom kept me home from school until the swelling in my lip went down, but she told Dad she was afraid I'd swallowed it."

"And then?"

"And then the next day I met Brody." Jess smiled and ached all at the same time. She missed him so much it burned within her. "Can you tell me where he is, George? Please? Some bit of news about him?"

George frowned. "Not yet."

"I see." Jess's shoulders slumped with disappointment. "Can I at least ask you something? Something else totally off topic that's been bothering me?"

"I can't guarantee I'll answer it."

"I understand." She laid it out anyway. "How long have you been a doctor?"

"Thirty-two years."

"So, is photography just a hobby?"

George looked around at the prints on his wall. "It is a hobby, yes. More of a passion, actually. A release."

"Did you stop being a doctor to work for the magazine?"

George looked bewildered. "Magazine?"

Jess peered at George as if he were the crazy one. "Yes, Starlight Fashion Magazine. I worked with you three times a week before school. You taught me everything I know."

Scribble-scribble.

Jess realized she was getting no answers when George didn't avert his eyes from his page and said, "So, after you met Brody … then what?"

Jess was getting better at suppressing the rage that welled within her. And when she eyed the letter opener on George's desk she realized that made him a lucky, lucky man.

****

The meetings with George continued daily. Weeks turned into months. Jess was able to squeeze out very little information from George, and he adapted quickly to her attempts to ruse. Her dad would visit, and he, too, was tight lipped. Jess figured after his initial bombshell George was keeping him on a short leash.

She had one spark of hope when she'd asked Carter Benson who the Giants' rookie catcher was when they won the World Series. She expected to hear the name Brody Campbell, but her heart sank when he had mentioned some guy she'd never heard of named Buster Posey, and how it was a shame he missed almost the whole next season with a broken leg.

George continued to pry memories from her with his semi-hypnotic technique, and Jess continued to fill in some of the gaps by using it herself. Jess was growing more and more impatient with George, however, as he continually asked her to retrieve the wrong memories. He was asking her to pull images of times when things were good, trying to make her remember that her life wasn't that bad. She wanted him to know her mother drank like a fish and hit like a pimp. She wanted him to know at least some of the pain she felt as a child.

Then one day the would-be twin of her bus driver didn't take the left turn to lead her to George's office, but continued forward toward music and voices.

"George said you'd earned a little Common Room time." The nurse put the brakes on the chair and led her to a soft recliner on the edge of a room half full of other patients.

"What is this place?"

"Oh, just a place to watch TV or visit with your family or talk to other patients. Just some place you can go so you're not stuck in your bed all day."

Jess surveyed the room briefly, and she had the weirdest feeling of déjà vu.

Her eyes fell upon a bald guy that was covered in piercings and tattoos. He was rocking back and forth in his chair and punching the wall as he cursed out loud.

"He … he used to ride my bus." Jess's voice came out in a squeak.

"He what, honey?"

Jess pointed. "That guy right there. He used to ride the same bus I rode from work to school. The one … the one your twin used to drive."

She examined the remaining occupants in the room and saw another group she could identify from the bus: a woman staring blankly ahead of her at nothing, an older child holding a younger child beside her, the middle child, eyes red-rimmed and puffy, snot caked around her nostrils, trying to get her mother's attention, but it was all in vain.

Mom was out of it.

Jess sat back in her chair and fretted over how coincidental all this was. The nurse wasn't her bus driver. The patients weren't passengers.

And that music.

The music that resonated through the Common Room.

That stupid big band music they were forced to listen to on the city bus.

The common room *was* the city bus.

Jess stood. "I need to see George. Now."

Chapter Twenty-One

Jess stormed into George's office, but stopped short of his desk and breathed deeply to calm herself when she saw him brace for an attack. After a few seconds he apparently realized she wasn't going to rip out his throat with her index finger, and relaxed his grip on the arms of his chair.

"What can I do for you, Jess?" His voice quavered a bit.

"George, I need to know. I've spent months telling you everything about me. Now I need *you* to tell me about me. I need to know. I'm ready to know."

George nodded. "Sit down."

Jess sat, still consciously breathing deeply. In through the nose. Out through the mouth. Her anger was bubbling at her kneecaps, and she was fighting to keep it from rising higher. She watched his facial expressions, and he appeared to be toiling over how to proceed.

"You are not twenty-three years old," he said finally.

Jess cocked her head to the left as a dog does when it's trying to understand its master. "I'm … I'm not?"

"No, you're not."

Awkward silence ensued. Jess wasn't exactly sure she wanted the answers she had so desperately longed for a few short minutes ago. Finally her curiosity won out. "Well, how old am I?"

"You are sixteen, Jess. You'll be seventeen next month."

Jess did the math in her head. "So, when I first saw you—when I … attacked you—I was sixteen and it *was* May like I'd said."

"Yes."

"But you told me I'd been here seven years. How can I have been here for seven years and still be sixteen?"

"The reason your voice sounded different to you when you awoke was because the last time you heard it was right before you were institutionalized. You were brought here when you were nine years old."

The fury rose from her kneecaps to her elbows in one swift surge. "How is that possible? I've lived the past seven years at home with my dad. I've grown up. I've gone to school. I've … I've had sex."

George raised his now healed eyebrow. Some of the white tufts of hair grew at odd angles due to the scarring beneath. "Sex?"

"Yes. Brody and I had sex the night I … the night I realized I'd … I'd killed my mother."

George chuckled. "He was trying to hold on to the very end, wasn't he?"

Jess was confused. "What do you mean?"

"Do you know why you came here?"

"Yes. I killed my mother. We've established that." Jess was becoming impatient. The rage bubbled a little at her elbows, but remained where it was. She reminded herself to breathe. In through the nose. Out through the mouth.

George leaned forward. "You were my patient two years prior to that episode, Jess."

"What?" The fire within her now smoldered at her shoulders.

"You've been coming to see me since you were seven. I know you remembered your longing to have a picture on my wall. How could you have done that if you were hospitalized? How did you know me prior to your incarceration?"

Jess thought about it, and she had no explanation other than to believe him. "Why did I have to come see you, George?" This was another question she wasn't sure she wanted answered, and her anger settled at her neckline in anticipation.

"Your parents were concerned over several issues, so they brought you to me."

"Several issues?" Breathe in. Breathe out.

"Your father was concerned over the fact you were such a Tomboy, though your mother actually embraced it."

Yes, Jess thought. Embraced it because Tomboys are much more apt to be injured than regular girls. She tasted the fury in her mouth, hot and putrid like rotting flesh, and she suppressed the urge to vomit.

"But the main issue was something different," he continued.

"What something different?" In. Out. In. Out. Faster and faster.

George appeared to examine Jess and evaluate her temper. "I think I've said enough for one day, Jess. You have plenty to think about before we meet tomorrow."

"I don't think so, *George*." When she stood, the anger reached the top of her head and she remembered nothing else.

****

Jess awoke to darkness and instant fear of what she'd done to George when she'd blacked out. She reviewed the office in her mind and remembered the letter opener on his desk, and her stomach flopped uncomfortably. She figured she could use his memory recall technique as she had in the past, but then her body

179

curled into a ball against her will as other thoughts took over, overwhelming her with grief and worry and disbelief all at once.

The seven years of her life she thought she'd lost were still to come, but the past seven she'd thought she'd lived were fallacy. She had believed she had gone to high school and worked as a Photographer's Assistant with George as her boss and Brody Campbell as her boyfriend whom she loved dearly and still yearned for with every beat of her heart.

She'd believed it like God's honest truth and she would have sworn to it on a stack of bibles.

But she'd have been wrong.

A soft knock at her door caused her to unfurl and discover her face was bathed in tears and snot. The door opened and George entered, visibly undamaged, to Jess's relief.

"I was here late and I wanted to check in on you." He handed her a box of tissues.

"I'm just so … confused, George." Her body continued its sobbing despite her desire to quit. "How did all of this happen? What has my body been doing the past seven years while my mind was living an imaginary life?"

George slid the chair over by her bed and sat down. "You have been catatonic for most of it. The police found you at the scene with your mother and at first they believed you'd merely witnessed her murder and not perpetrated it. It took them several weeks to put the pieces together. But your father had you brought here immediately, as you were already in my care. After they figured you'd done it, it was agreed you'd stay here."

"I was already in your care," Jess said snidely. "Nice work." She regretted her words instantly, and apologized at once.

"I don't blame you, Jess. It's true I didn't understand the depths of your jealousy."

"My … my *what*?" Jealousy?

"After talking to your parents and talking to you, I deduced you were severely jealous of your mother. Not only over her beauty, but also over the attention she drew from your father."

"You deduced that, did you?" Jess had to grit her teeth to avoid saying anything else, and tears of remorse quickly became tears of disbelief.

"Yes. You dressed as a boy and played sports as a boy in attempt to regain your father's approval."

Jess held her tongue.

"And then when your mother became pregnant, it only heightened the envy within you. You feared you already had so little attention from your father, a baby would only detract from it more."

That was the last straw. "You are incorrect."

George looked at her in an oh-really-and-who-has-the-degree-on-his-wall sort of way. "I am incorrect?"

"Way off base, George."

"Then I should ignore your use of baseball analogies?"

Jess rolled her eyes. "I'm not allowed to like baseball 'cause I'm a girl?"

"You're allowed to like baseball. As long as it's a healthy like, Jess. If you like it only to gain the affections of your father, that's not healthy."

"George, have you totally ignored the fact that my mother repeatedly beat the piss out of me? That she drank like a fish? That she blamed me for her stretch marks and never let me forget I was the reason she no longer had a modeling career? Haven't I told you this over and over? Haven't I filled you in on these details? I'm sure you've probably gone back and gotten the hospital reports to corroborate my stories?"

George rifled through the thick file. "There were hospital reports, yes. But your parents and the doctors all agreed they were accidents."

"Accidents." Jess's body went numb.

"Yes, Jess. You were a rough Tomboy involved in sports. You fell often and skinned your knees. You were regularly bumped and bruised, even occasionally broken. But it was always explained."

"Why don't you believe me, George?"

"Because you're still hanging on, Jess. You're still stuck where you were when you first came to see me so many years ago. I commend you for being able to stifle your anger and your violent tendencies, but you're still blaming your mother for your illness. You're still lying to me."

"But I'm not lying to you, George. I'm not." Jess was ashamed of the tears as they fell from her eyes. She wanted to remain strong, but she couldn't understand why George didn't believe her. And then a light clicked. She finally got it. She finally realized. Brody. She'd known Brody before she'd been brought there. Brody always knew. Brody was always there to hold her when she needed it. Brody always said grownups wouldn't believe her about her mother's abuse. Brody always told her how to explain away the bruises. "Brody always told me you'd never understand."

George frowned. "And I've told you before—you should never pay attention to your imaginary friend."

"My ... my *what*?"

"Your imaginary friend, Jess. As in fictional. As in fabricated. As in fake. As in Brody Campbell."

KIM HARNES

Chapter Twenty-Two

Jess wrung the crisp white sheet in her hands as if strangling the shit out of it would somehow transfer itself to George's throat and he would suffer for what he'd just said. The rage seared within her from her toes to her fingertips. It burned the backs of her eyes and spit out fresh angry tears that spilled down her cheeks.

"Why would you tell me this, George? Why?"

"Because it's true, Jess. You created Brody when you were seven. That's why your parents put you in my care."

Impossible. That was utter nonsense. No way, no how. Jess's heart broke audibly into a million pieces. "You're lying."

"It is very important you believe me, Jess. It's important for your recovery."

Jess showed him the leather cord looping her wrist. "What about this, George? I made this for him. He wore it all the time. He never took it off."

"Jess, you made that here in the Common Room with one of the nurses one day after a session while I talked to your mother. You are the one who never took it off."

"But when I met Brody there were other people there. How could that happen if he weren't real?"

"What other people, Jess?"

Jess began to recall her memory of the lunchroom encounter with Brody and the other girl with the fancy dress and the flaming red hair while George looked at her with interest.

"Well, don't you see?" he said when she was finished. "Both of those girls were you, Jess."

"What?" She didn't think she had heard him correctly.

"They were both you. One of you was the Princess and one of you was the Tomboy and you let him choose which one of you you'd continue to be."

"But … But why would I do such a thing? Why would I create an imaginary friend?"

"Well, as I said before, you were very jealous."

Jess seethed every time she heard him say that.

"My findings were that you created Brody as a way to make up for where you felt your father was lacking in his attention toward you. You made him to like baseball and be involved in what your father would have been involved with. And he helped you create horrible stories about your mother."

Jess stared daggers at George. Brody didn't help her create stories about her mother. He helped create excuses to cover up her injuries because no one believed her when she told the truth about them, anyway. "No," Jess said again. "It can't be. Brody is real."

"Then where is he now, Jess?"

"I don't know! Nobody will tell me! You won't let anyone tell me *anything*!" Jess could feel the mercury rising with her hatred.

"You've made great strides in your treatment *because* of that reason, Jess. Well, that and your medication combined with your willingness to heal. If I had told you Brody didn't exist three months ago you'd have bitten off more than my eyebrow." He raised his damaged brow as an exhibition of her capabilities.

Jess stared at the twisted mess of bed sheet in her hands. "This is all wrong, George. All wrong."

"I can understand why you'd feel that way. I've listened to you tell me your story from the beginning.

You've told me of a life you believed was real—a life you thought you'd lived and you hadn't. Yet some of the people within that life are actually real people that you know from this hospital, right? How could the woman who has been your nurse for the past three years also be your bus driver, Jess? How could you have known Carter Benson from high school if you were never there? How could you have ridden the bus four months ago with bald, tattooed Chaz Moline if he's been in this hospital for the past year and a half?"

But Jess had no answers to any of George's questions. Either she was lying or he was, and she figured since she was the only one who had recently been in a straitjacket, the odds were not in her favor.

"Tell me more," she said finally. "About the truth. About what's real."

"All in due time, Jess." George patted her knee and stood. "We'll talk more tomorrow."

Jess's heart sank in contrast to her anger, which had only continued to grow until it was screaming in both her ears. "I don't want to talk tomorrow. I want to talk now!"

"It's late. You need to get some rest."

"I don't want rest, George. I want answers."

George appeared to eye her inquisitively. "Answers will come, Jess. They may not come as fast as you'd like, but these things take time."

"Time." Jess looked at her surroundings—he bright white walls of a hospital room in a Psychiatric ward. She certainly wasn't going anywhere anytime soon. Time was definitely something she had.

Time. Lots and lots of time.

****

"Time to get up, J-Bird!"

Jess rolled over and pulled the covers up over her head. She didn't want to get up.

"C'mon, Jess! It's a beautiful day!" The curtains opened spilling sunlight upon her bed. She could see the brightness even through her blankets and closed eyes.

"Daddy! I don't wanna!"

"Come on, J-Bird! One quick visit with George and then we're off to the ballpark for your championship game!"

Jess rolled over and turned her back against the sunlit window. "How about I just sleep another hour and go straight to the game?"

Wesley chuckled. "Come on, Jess. I think you really want to go see George today."

"Brody says he doesn't like it when I go see George. Brody said George doesn't like him and he doesn't think Brody should be my friend."

"George wants what's best for you and so do I."

Jess sat up and let the covers fall. "But Brody is best for me." She grinned and her dad seemed helpless to resist. He scooped her up in his arms and swung her around the room.

"Well, what's best for you right now is getting out of those pajamas and into your uniform. You've got a big day!"

Jess giggled and snuggled into her dad's embrace. "I love you, Daddy."

"I love you, too, Jess."

Her dad put her down and she went to her dresser to search for her uniform, but was unable to find it. She quickly made her way to her closet, but it wasn't hanging there, either.

"Dad?"

"Yeah, Jess?" His voice echoed down the hallway.

"Where's my uniform?" She frantically rifled through all her drawers and ravaged through her closet a second time with the same negative result.

"It isn't in your room?"

"No!" Jess could hear the complaint in the tone of her voice and instantly knew what that would bring.

"Jessica, you stop whining this instant!"

Jess heard her mother's footsteps tromp heavily down the hallway toward her room and she cowered from the noise. She reached for the hair at her temple and began to twist, encircling her finger with the sound of each step as it resonated through the floor.

"What seems to be the problem?" The plume of smoke preceded her entrance, and Jess heard the ice cubes tinkle against the side of her glass of what she claimed to be orange juice.

She looked at her mother with eyes larger than saucers and feared for what would come. "I ... I can't find my uniform."

"Where did you put it last?"

"Um ... I think in the laundry basket."

"Did you wash it?"

"No."

"Then it's probably still in the laundry basket."

Jess braced herself for the hit, and was surprised and relieved when her mother merely pivoted on her heel and left the room, leaving a toxic cloud of smoke billowing behind her. Jess slowly made her way to the laundry room, fished her dirty, holey uniform out of the basket, wincing as she inhaled the polluted stink of several games' worth of grass and dirt and sweat, and *got dressed. She made sure to stuff her mitt and bat into her duffel bag, and trudged to the car. She looked glumly at the clouds and wished really hard that her game wouldn't be called due to rain. Baseball was all she had. Well, baseball and Brody.*

They pulled into the hospital parking lot and followed the maze of hallways to George's office. Jess glanced at the entwined hands of her mother and father clasped together tightly in consolation, and she wondered why no one was attempting to comfort her. It was her appointment, after all.

Anger crept into her spine and traveled outward.

When they entered George's office, however, the anger dissipated and joy replaced it. A new photograph donned his wall, and it was hers. George had decorated it with a big white bow and he was standing beside it.

"It's a beautiful picture, Jess. And very therapeutic."

"Thera-puke what?"

George laughed. "Therapeutic. It means it is good for you."

Jess scrunched up her nose because she didn't understand what George meant. "Huh?"

"The picture, Jess. It's the perfect image of a butterfly coming out of its cocoon. And it's like you coming out of where you were into where you need to be."

Jess looked curiously at George. "Huh?" she said again.

"The butterfly is you. And you were trapped in this cocoon. But you escaped. And you're free. And you're much better for it. Look how beautiful you are."

Jess still didn't understand, but nobody had ever called her beautiful before, so she smiled. "Thanks, George," she said, and made her way to her usual chair.

George took his place behind his desk. "Whatever are you wearing, Jessica?"

"Jess," she corrected.

"Sorry, whatever are you wearing, Jess?"

Jess looked down at herself. "My baseball uniform."

"Don't you like to have it washed?"

Jess was instantly ashamed over her shabby appearance.

"She just loves that one," her mother piped in. "She has three clean ones in her closet, but I just can't keep her out of that scraggly thing."

George looked at Amanda and smiled. "Superstition?"

"Exactly."

Jess glared at her mother, but she was pretty sure nobody noticed.

"Well, that does happen, doesn't it?" George looked at Jess pitifully. Jess frothed with anger at all three of them: her mother with her excuses, George for believing them, and her father for ignoring it all.

Jess looked to her left and smiled when she saw Brody, her friend, standing quietly in the room with them in his crisp, white uniform with no holes. His voice was barely louder than a whisper so only she could hear. "Don't listen to him, Jess," he said. "And don't say anything. Telling George about your mom will only make things worse. They won't believe you and they'll only try to keep you away from me. And then you won't have anybody to talk to. No one else understands what you're *going through the way I understand what you're going through."*

Jess didn't want to be kept from Brody. Brody was nice to her. Brody listened to her when her mother hit her. Brody calmed her when she was angry. Brody made her smile when she didn't think she could. Brody made her happy.

Jess turned away from her photograph on the wall and she smiled at George in her stinky uniform.

When Jess awoke she was tormented and upset.

He truly wasn't real. He couldn't have been, or he wouldn't have been unable to go unnoticed by anyone but her in that office. No one else could see or hear him.

Brody was the one who said she couldn't tell George her mother was horrible. Maybe if she'd told the truth back then, she'd have a leg to stand on. Some backstory. Some evidence. Should she blame Brody because no one believed her now?

Her anger simmered and she wasn't sure where it was aimed.

She didn't know who deserved the blame.

But now neither her mother nor Brody existed.

Jess buried her face in her hands and cried.

Chapter Twenty-Three

As the days and weeks and months dragged by, Jess was able to piece together more of how her real life intermingled with her imaginary one. Several more of the passengers from her bus turned up in the common area as patients. They were lifeless and placid and mostly just sat there staring at their own imaginary worlds within them. The school nurse was actually the nurse at the reception area checking in new patients and asking them to "tell the truth, Mr. Whomever," about whether or not they'd done any type of illegal drug. More and more of her classmates manifested themselves as janitors, nurses and orderlies. More and more of her teachers turned out to be doctors and security guards.

And to her mounting dismay, none of them was Brody.

Jess figured out more, as well. Subtle things. One of the doctors drove a metallic blue 1967 Chevy Impala and always parked it outside her window. Her own room in the hospital was Room 228. One of the orderlies, obese and greasy-haired and pockmarked and who usually eyed her hesitantly, always smelled of salami and mustard or burgers and mustard or something with mustard, and occasionally wore Brody's "date" cologne. When he would walk by she would breathe in a little deeper than usual and close her eyes and see Brody's face, even for just a second.

And that made her smile.

The episodes of déjà vu she'd imagined in her world were actually shadows of what she was really living: the glimpse of George in a lab coat in the hallway, the white walls of her hospital room instead of the green walls of her bedroom, the flash of what she'd initially surmised to be her mother in the mirror, but later gathered was actually her own withered and ghost-like reflection. And until just recently someone showed up at two o'clock every afternoon and at two o'clock every morning to administer her medicine. She was thankful at least that for the past few months they'd begun to give her capsules to swallow morning and night instead of using her ass as a pin cushion, but Jess didn't think it was coincidence that when she'd received the injections, it just happened to be the same times Brody's "whatever it was" in his head was at its worst. It was the medicine that had caused it. Along with its providing the realization of what she'd done to her mother, the medicine was also killing Brody slowly inside her mind.

And some small part of Jess hated everyone for that.

Her visits with George were uneventful. As long as she didn't talk about Brody or about her mother's violent abuse or mammoth consumption of alcohol, George seemed thrilled with her progress. When he would ask about her mother, she would either claim to not remember, or pretend she was jealous of her, because that was what she believed he wanted, and that seemed to satisfy him.

And that brought out the anger from within her.

When her dad would come to visit, their conversations were limited to how his day had gone at work, what the ever-changing weather was doing in an outside world she barely truly remembered, and what he'd managed to burn for dinner. And she smiled and laughed because that was what was expected of her.

And that disgusted her. It repulsed her. And yet, there was nothing she could do about it because she was where she was and they were where they were.

So outside she was happy and complacent and saying all the right things. And inside her fury roiled like flames in the pit of hell. And she was pretty sure that wasn't good.

She was pretty sure that wasn't good at all.

Especially when one autumn afternoon George announced, "I've got some good news for you." He closed her chart on his desk and folded his hands over it.

"What good news?" Jess eyed him suspiciously.

George smiled. "I think you're ready to go home."

"You … you think I'm *what*?"

Apparently that wasn't the reaction George was anticipating. "Don't you want to go home?"

Did she? She wasn't exactly sure. She didn't think she really knew what home was anymore. Would her dad even want her back? "Where will I stay?"

George chuckled. "Well, with your father, silly. You're only seventeen. Where did you think you were going to go?"

"I actually never thought I was getting out of here."

George smiled. "Well, if you don't want to go, I won't make you go. If you're going to be uncomfortable, you can still stay here."

"No, no. I want to go." And she realized after she'd said it that it was true. She wanted some sense of normalcy to balance out the chaos in her head.

"I'll get the discharge papers ready, and your dad will be here to pick you up first thing tomorrow morning."

"Okay." Jess waited in anticipation for what would come next, sure there would be plenty of restrictions and conditions.

"But there will be rules."

Ah, yes.

"First, you still have to come see me. Every day, for a while. Less and less if I feel you're progressing well."

Jess nodded. She didn't like it, but she didn't have a choice.

"And you will take your medication like clockwork."

Jess nodded again.

"For the time being, no television, no radio, no books, nothing of the outside world."

She looked down at her hands. That certainly didn't leave her with a lot of options of what she could actually do.

"I'm going to reiterate these instructions to your father so it is very clear what I expect of both of you before your release."

Jess nodded for a third and final time.

"Okay, then." George clapped his hands together in dismissal. "My office tomorrow morning at nine. Your dad knows to be here."

Jess was led back to her room, no longer requiring a chair for transport. "Are you excited to go home?" The bus-driver-nurse was smiling a sad sort of smile.

"I'm not sure, I guess," Jess answered truthfully. "I don't think it's had time to sink in yet." And it certainly hadn't.

"Well, I know you don't really know me all that well, Honey, but I'm gonna miss taking care of you and taking you from place to place."

Jess wasn't exactly sure how to respond to that, so she just smiled up at her and that seemed to be enough.

When Jess returned to her room she leaned back against her board-like pillows, still dumbstruck over her release. It wasn't that she didn't *want* to leave her lumpy, strap-laden bed surrounded by the cold, white walls of the hospital and replace it with her soft, warm bed with the cool green walls in the bedroom of the house she loved and remembered. She was also pretty sure she could handle *not* running into people on the inside that she thought she'd known on the outside—or was that vice versa? — The most recent of which turned out to be Pickle, who was wearing food-stained light green scrubs and speaking with George about the menu for Thanksgiving dinner.

Yet, the thought of leaving the hospital consumed her with fear – a newer, less common emotion as opposed to the rage that was usually always at the brink of boiling over.

The hospital was shelter. It was comfort and sanctuary. It was everything home should have been for her. And, she assumed, it was everything home could be for her again.

A knock on the door brought her out of her internal deliberation, and the large and pockmarked orderly entered with fresh linens, which he set on the counter. "Getting outta here tomorrow, eh?" It was the first time she'd heard his unpleasantly high-pitched, nasally voice, but his breath smelled blessedly once again of salami with mustard.

"Yeah." Jess smiled feebly.

"What's-a-matter? Don't you want to go home?"

Jess resisted the urge to grab the hair at her temple, and twisted the leather strap around her wrist instead. "I guess I don't really know. I don't know anything else but this, do I?"

"Do … do you remember anything? Like … from when you were out of it?"

"Not really."

"You'll get the hang of it." He smiled. "These are for when you leave." He motioned to the sheets he'd brought in. "I figured I'd get them ready ahead of time and Carter can change them in the morning after you've gone."

"Thanks." It was an awkward thing to say, Jess thought. Why would she be thanking him for that? Still, she thought she should say something.

"Actually …" His voice lowered to just above a whisper. "I really just came in to say goodbye."

"Well, I'll be back in every day for a while to see George."

"I guess I'll see you around, huh?"

"Sure, you will," Jess said. He smiled and turned to leave, but turned back abruptly when Jess cried, "Wait!"

"What is it?"

She stood and approached him, her bare feet noiselessly caressing the linoleum floor. She took the collar of his shirt in her hands, buried her face in his chest, and breathed in deeply. She went back to bed without a word, letting his exhilarating smell enter her lungs and permeate her body, and she barely heard the door snap closed when he left.

Jess curled her knees into her body, closed her eyes, and tried to imagine Brody's face.

****

"Hi, Beautiful."
"Brody?"
"Yes. It's me."

Jess searched through the dark but couldn't see anything. "I can't find you, Brody. Where are you?"

"I'm right here. I can't stay long. I miss you."

Jess cried. "I miss you, too. But you're not real. George told me everything."

"Is this real?"

Jess still couldn't see him, but she could smell his cologne. She could feel his soft caress on her cheek as he wiped her tears away.

She reached for him, but he wasn't there. "I can't find you."

"I'm right here." And his voice was inside her head. "Right here."

KIM HARNES

Chapter Twenty-Four

Jess looked out the window of a car she'd never ridden in, adorned in clothes she'd never worn, at an apartment building she'd never been to. "Here we are." Wesley Waterford put the car in park and opened his door.

"What do you mean, 'here we are'? Where's our house?"

Her dad looked at his lap. "I guess I should have warned you ahead of time. I sold the house six years ago. It was too large for just me and it had too many memories."

Jess's heart sank when images of her dad happily decorating a nursery flashed across her mind and guilt overpowered both fear and anger within her.

"Anyway, when George told me you got to come home, I cleaned all my extra crap out of the spare bedroom and made it up for you. I think you'll like it." He smiled despite the thick furrows in his forehead, and Jess returned it despite her own.

They exited the car, climbed three flights of stairs, and walked halfway down a hallway until her dad stopped at a door and took keys out of his pocket, the jangle of metal against metal making a sickening noise that reminded her of her captivity. He unlocked the door and opened it for her with a flourish. "Welcome to your new home."

Jess walked timidly inside the small living room and eyed the shabby furniture and worn carpet. Nothing was the same. The cozy couch she remembered was gone. The recliner her dad had always sat in was gone. She recognized nothing except one picture—a portrait of her provocatively posed, half-naked mother larger than the television it hung above—and she cringed at the revulsion that coursed through her at the sight of it. She thought her dad had gotten rid of that picture, but realized it was only part of the world within her mind where it no longer existed. She was afraid to open her mouth for fear of the vomit that would escape, so she spoke through clenched teeth. "Where's my room?"

He apparently failed to notice her discomfort, or chose to ignore it, as he continued with his grandiose behavior. "Right this way!" He led her past the tiny kitchen toward a short hallway with two doors on one side and one on the other. "Bathroom." He pointed to the first door on the right. "My room." He pointed to the door on the left. "Your room." And he opened the second door on the right.

Jess entered the room and almost tripped over the bed.

She heard her dad clear his throat behind her. "Sorry. I know it's smaller than what you're used to."

She surveyed the undersized space: a twin bed, a stacked 6-drawer dresser, and an empty little stand that she figured should have held a television but didn't (probably George's idea, she thought). There was barely enough space to maneuver in the room, which was no bigger than her mother's walk-in closet had been in the old house. "It's fine," she said, just the same.

Her dad smiled halfheartedly, as though he knew she was only trying to appease him, which, of course, she was.

"Well, why don't you unpack and we'll have some lunch?" Wesley clapped his hands together.

Jess looked at him inquisitively. "Um, Dad … I don't have anything to unpack."

He was obviously embarrassed. "Sorry." He looked at the threadbare carpet. "Maybe I should go get you some clothes?"

"You?" Jess asked. "Or us?"

Wesley appeared to look at a bald patch in the carpet, and he toed it absentmindedly with his shoe to avoid her gaze. "Me," he answered.

Jess understood. She was free from the hospital, yes, but she'd jumped from one form of imprisonment into a new one—a supposedly freer, yet smaller one. One that was nothing like she'd remembered and nothing that felt like home in any way, shape, or form.

All in good time, she thought.

"Don't get me anything pink," she said finally.

"Forever the Tomboy." Wesley touched his daughter's face. "But you look *so* like your mother."

Jess went rigid. Of all the things he could possibly say to her, that was the worst. She knew it was true, though. In her world she'd imagined herself as ordinary and plain and having the characteristics of her father's side of the family. When she'd awakened into the real world and had seen her reflection for the first time, she thought her mother had come back to haunt her. But it was her own gaunt and blood-covered face looking back at her. And she wanted to scratch it off.

She glared at the back of her dad's head as he turned and left through the door.

Jess wandered aimlessly through the apartment all afternoon, trying to avoid the living room's gigantic picture of her mother, as well as any mirrors. She knew not to listen to the radio, watch television, or use the phone. Who was she going to call, really?

Yet she continued to eye the receiver on the coffee table. What if? What if she picked it up and dialed Brody's number and he was there?

Ridiculousness.

But still.

She inched closer, feeling the portrait of her mother sting her as she entered the room. But what harm could it do? What harm could *she* do?

Curiosity won out and she picked up the handset and dialed. She waited in anticipation for the voice on the other end.

"Big Five Sporting Goods. This is Matt."

Wrong voice. "Hi. Um … May I speak with Brody Campbell, please?"

"Brody who?"

"Campbell." Jess already knew what was coming next.

"Sorry. Nobody here by that name."

She set the earpiece in its cradle and dropped to the floor, her knees no longer containing the strength to hold her up. So, *that's* what harm she could do. She curled into a ball and sobbed.

And yearned.

And ached.

Jess didn't know just how long she'd been on the floor, but she was still there when her father returned. "J-Bird?" She heard his keys and packages drop to the floor in a metallic-paper-plastic thud. "Shit, J-Bird." He knelt beside her, his knees audibly popping just by her ear. "Jess?"

She didn't want to react. She didn't want to move. She didn't want to *be*.

"C'mon, Jess. Get up." Wesley put his arms beneath her and lifted her nearly weightless frame up and onto the couch. "I should never have left you alone so soon. I'm so, so sorry."

Jess buried her face into her dad's shoulder and continued to weep.

"Do you need me to call George?"

Though she wanted nothing more than to be back in the refuge of the hospital—to be free of the freeness that felt nothing like free—she shook her head no. She didn't want to fail. At anything. And returning to the hospital after mere hours of autonomy was something she was not able to accept. She would give it another go. She would try harder. She would succeed. "No," she said with more emphasis than she felt. "No, Daddy. I'm fine."

Wesley brushed the hair back away from her face. "You do look so like your mother," he said for the second time that day.

Maybe he needed to say it for his own reassurance. Maybe he thought she'd want to know she resembled her mother, the model. Maybe he thought she'd appreciate that he loved her despite what she'd done to his wife and unborn child. No matter what the reason, the flames rose within her, hurried and hot, and she quickly buried her face in her dad's chest again so he wouldn't see the revulsion cross her mom-like face.

"Is that what it is, Jess? Did you come in here and see the picture of your mother and that's what upset you?"

Jess quickly nodded yes. No, it wasn't why. No, it wasn't close. No, it wasn't even fair. But at this point, she didn't care what was fair. And maybe now she'd won this battle. Maybe now he'd take the fucking thing down.

****

205

One unintentional but well received victory later, Jess sat next to her dad on the couch. She stared at the blank space on the wall where her mother's vile portrait had hung, the Cheshire grin hidden beneath the afghan she curled under. She felt a small pang of guilt over how her father probably felt about having to take it down, but quickly dismissed it. This was, after all, helping her heal.

"Did you take your medicine?"

He had put two orange and white capsules in a little ceramic dish shaped like a butterfly on the side of the bathroom sink, and she had gulped them both down after she'd put on her pajamas and brushed her teeth. "Yes, Daddy."

"Good girl."

Anger, jealousy and resentment were at bay, and satisfaction took over.

Jess closed her eyes.

Chapter Twenty-Five

Jess opened her eyes as wide as they could go and strained not to blink for fear she'd miss something amazing. She'd never been to AT&T Park, and wanted to take in every inch of it. Happiness consumed her whole body and she thought she'd burst from within when the San Francisco Giants took the field.

"This okay, Jess?" Her dad handed her a huge tub of popcorn.

"Dad, this is SO awesome!" Jess stuffed a handful of salty, buttery deliciousness into her mouth and washed it down with a straw full of soda. Thankfully, though her mother was with them, she sat on the other side of her dad, and was mostly obscured. Jess wondered why she would wear such a short skirt and skimpy top and all that makeup to a baseball game, anyway, and she almost laughed out loud when she imagined her mother trying to aerate the grass in the outfield with her spiked heels and leave the little clumps on top that looked like goose turds. Jess thought that would at least have put them to better use, and she rubbed the sore spot on the top of her foot in remembrance of how she'd already used them that morning.

Bad thoughts pushed aside, she looked out over home plate and watched the game commence. She wished Brody could have been there, but her dad had said this was a family trip for her birthday, and she and Brody could do something together after they got back to Reno if she still wanted to. This was time for her to spend with her parents. Time for them to be together.

"God, these seats are uncomfortable, Wes."

Jess went rigid with disgust at the sound of her mother's voice, and she hoped her protesting wouldn't lead to their early departure from her first ever, professional baseball game. But when Jess's dad returned with a seat cushion, she relaxed a bit.

But Amanda wasn't through.

"I'm hungry." Wesley bought her a hotdog.

"I'm thirsty." Wesley brought her a beer.

"Is that all they have? Beer?" And Wesley returned with another drink of some sort that seemed to satiate her for the time being.

But then later on, "I'm cold." And Wesley left once again and came back with a blanket. Jess had thought at that moment that if her mother were wearing more clothes, she wouldn't be cold at all.

Each time her dad left to accommodate her mother's next wish, the space between them was vacant, allowing Jess to feel her mother's stare burn through her. Jess never looked, though. She tried hard to concentrate on the field and on the players and on the ball.

Jess felt badly for her father. She knew he wanted to watch the game just as much as she had, but she also knew he wanted to make Jess happy that day, and he was going to do everything he could to help her enjoy herself. Of course, after thinking that, she thought maybe they could have just left her mother at home and they'd have both had a good time.

This time when he returned with another drink for her mother, he turned to Jess and smiled, and then put her very own official MLB San Francisco Giants cap on her scraggly little head.

"Happy Birthday, J-Bird."

Jess pulled the cap off slowly and took it in both hands. She ran her fingertips over the orange and black embroidery and squeezed the brim. Then she looked back

*at her dad and returned his smile with a huge grin.
"Thanks, Daddy!"*

*"You're welcome." He sat back in his chair and
put his hand on Amanda's knee. "So, do you think the
Giants are gonna win for your birthday?"*

*Jess grinned. "We'll come back, Dad. I know we
will. I want to see a walk-off home run!"*

"Wow! That's asking for a lot!"

"They can do it. I know they can."

*Amanda stood abruptly. "Where's a person
supposed to smoke in this hell hole?"*

"You have to go—"

*"Why don't you just show me instead of explain it
to me?"*

"I can't leave Jess here alone."

"Well, bring it with us."

*"Amanda, I can't make her miss the game. It's
her birthday."*

*"I'll find it myself, then. If I don't come back, it's
because I've found someone else who actually
appreciates me." She swatted her own ass. "And this."
She shoved Wesley, stomped squarely on Jess's toe with
her stiletto causing her to squelch out in pain, and
stormed up the aisle.*

*Wesley looked back and forth between the top of
Jess's head and the backside of his wife. "J-Bird, I'm just
going to be gone ten minutes, okay?"*

*She didn't let her dad see the tears fall as she
nodded her head and heard him leave. Not even Jess was
sure if she were crying because of her crushed foot, or
her crumpled spirit. Not even baseball could make her
feel better now.*

Her mom had won.

"We left before the 7th inning stretch and listened to the rest of the game on the radio on the drive home." Jess was supine on George's couch.

"Is this something you've just remembered?" George scribbled on his notepad. "You hadn't mentioned this family birthday trip before."

"The cap. It was in an old box of baseball stuff my dad found."

"How did you feel about that?"

Jess sat up. "I was happy at first, because I loved that cap. I wore it all the time. My little league coach used to get mad because I wanted to wear it during games instead of the one that went with my uniform."

"And then?"

"And then I remembered how rotten my mother was during the game and how much she'd tried to ruin it for me."

"How did she try to ruin it for you?"

"You didn't just hear me explain how she complained through the whole thing and we finally left because of her?"

"No."

"What did you hear, George?"

"I heard a story of your parents trying to do something as a family for your birthday. Something they both knew you would enjoy immensely. Your mother may have been a bit uncomfortable, but she was doing her best to accommodate you and your wishes for your birthday by going along."

The flash of anger shot red across her eyes. "Yes. I guess you would see it that way."

George looked offended. "Why would you say that, Jess? I'm here to help you."

Another spark popped inside her. Jess wanted more than anything to be able to tell George it felt like he wasn't here to help her at all. It felt as though he were here to tell her how wonderful her mom was, when clearly that wasn't the case. As if he were here to make her feel guilty over how she'd misrepresented her mother's treatment of her. She wanted to jump up and scream into George's face that her mother was a horrible, terrible, manipulative bitch.

But she didn't. She couldn't. She wasn't allowed to because to him, that was lies. To him, that was detrimental to her recovery. That wasn't going to help her heal. Her last ditch effort to expose her mother's tyranny thwarted, she looked at the clock and saw she had only a few minutes left in her session and decided to change the subject. "George?"

"Yes, Jess."

"Why do I know things?"

George cocked his head to the side. "What do you mean?"

"Why am I not stupid?"

"You've never been stupid." He smiled.

"No, I mean why don't I talk like a nine-year-old? Why do I know things I shouldn't know? Why do I have a teenagers mind if I've never been a normal teenager? And how do I know about sex?"

George cleared his throat. "Well, most of that would be guessing on my part."

"So guess." She figured anything was better than the nothing she currently had.

"Well, you've already mentioned you've seen some of the same people in both worlds as well as some of the same items, cars, sounds, smells. Correct?"

"Yes."

"So, my theory is you were able to listen to those speak around you and learn from them. Your caretakers continued to talk to you during your stay here. I think you picked things up as you went along."

"But what about sex?"

George seemed to cringe a bit. "My guess on that is, whether your body experienced it or not, it was still changing. Your body still went through puberty and you still started your period and you still had the animal instinct for sexual feelings because that's what a teenage body does."

Jess pondered that for a moment and was silent. Could be, she thought. It certainly made some sense, at least. And she had no reason to think otherwise.

George put the cap on his pen and dropped it onto his writing pad. "Anything else?"

"What did I look like?"

"Well, you've always looked like your mother."

Annoyance wrenched her insides. "I mean when I was ... out of it. What did I do? How did I look?"

George shifted in his chair. "You mostly just sat there smiling."

"Smiling?"

"For the most part. Until we started to experiment with your medication and you began to come around."

"Well, what did I do then?"

"For a couple weeks you were fidgety and you cried and yelled and kicked, and twirled your hair a lot like you'd used to when you were younger. You even punched yourself in the nose and made it bleed."

Jess thought back to her unexplained nosebleed in class and realized that must have been what had caused it to happen: The connection between what was real, and what was imaginary.

"That's when we knew you were improving," George continued.

Improving. So, when she'd stopped smiling and had become angry and violent that's when they knew she was *better?* And now they're telling her to stop being angry and violent and smile again. It seemed to Jess while she was in her own world, she was happy. It was in the real world where everything sucked.

Maybe they should have taken the hint and let her stay where she was.

Maybe she'd still have had something to smile about.

And so most of the time anger bubbled within her and ate her up inside and tortured her mind and haunted her dreams. But happy was on her outside because that was what George and her father wanted. And every time she thought about what they wanted the anger boiled a little hotter—churned a little more within her – and melted away what little real happy she had left.

Jess went on and on for months with the same routine. Fall left and winter took its place. Then spring came and went. She continually grew better and better at presenting happy to George and her father, and they encouraged her progress. The other members of the hospital staff saw her happy and gushed over how well she looked and how pleased they were she was advancing so far in her therapy.

But every day was the same. Every single day.

She still saw George three times a week—every Monday, Wednesday, and Friday. She still wasn't allowed to do anything in public, listen to the radio, or watch television. Even when she remembered something about her mother she didn't tell George about it, and when he asked her to recall something specific, she'd leave out all the bad parts on purpose.

When she wasn't at the hospital, she sat at home and talked to her dad about nothing in particular. She showered and she dressed and she ate and she slept and she took her medicine like a good girl.

And things went on like that for quite some time.

And everyone was content.

And Jess's anger was buried where it was supposed to be and her happy was at the surface where it was expected.

And just as all things were right in the world, the world took a subtle turn.

Chapter Twenty-Six

Jess spit into the sink and rinsed off her toothbrush, avoiding her mom-like reflection in the medicine cabinet mirror as usual, but catching it in her periphery anyway. Distaste quickly consumed her entire being. She stuffed the toothbrush into its cup a little too brusquely causing it to teeter and fall over onto the ceramic butterfly on the edge of the sink and spilling its contents. Jess was able to catch one of the capsules, but watched helplessly as the other one was washed down the sink with tap water and toothpaste foam in an orange and white swirl.

"Oh, shit." Jess looked at the single pill in her hand, then back to the drain. It was gone.

Memories of a conversation she'd overheard between George and her father reverberated in her mind.

"Is there something else I can give her, George? Something else that will work the same?"

"Unfortunately, no. This is what she needs."

"But they're experimental. And my insurance won't cover them. Her hospitalization has already wiped me out."

"I wish there were something else."

Jess held back the tears. It was only one pill, she told herself. How expensive could one pill be? She'd just tell him she needed another one. But the more she thought of telling her father she'd lost one down the drain, the more she thought of how hard she'd been trying to not disappoint him, and how she didn't think she could stand to be scolded—even if it were just a disapproving look. She didn't know if she could handle it, and she was afraid if he did get upset at her, grief would overpower her and wipe away happy, or worse, anger would reach the surface and finally take over completely.

She eventually came to the realization that what he didn't know wouldn't hurt him. And it was, after all, only one pill, so that couldn't hurt her, either. And she'd take two of them tomorrow morning, right?

"Did you take your medicine yet, J-Bird?" Her dad's voice rang down the hallway.

"Just about to, Dad."

The small stitch of guilt aside, she popped the single orange and white capsule into her mouth and washed it down.

"I thought I heard a noise in here. Is everything okay?" Wesley was at the door startling Jess and making her jump.

"I'm fine." She began to pick the cup, the toothbrush, and the ceramic dish out of the sink and put them back into their respectable places, fearful he'd seen her only take half her medication. "Just got a little clumsy brushing my teeth."

"You're shaking, J-Bird." He reached out and pulled her into a hug. "Are you okay, Princess?"

He hadn't seen. Jess swallowed the lump in her throat and lied through her teeth. "Yes, Daddy."

"I recorded the Giants game. Do you want to watch?"

"I … I thought I wasn't allowed to." But oh, how she wanted to.

"I can fast forward through the commercials. I've already cleared it with George."

Jess beamed at her father.

"I'll take that as a yes."

Jess nodded so violently she almost gave herself whiplash.

Wesley laughed, lifted his daughter up over his shoulder, carried her down the hallway, and plopped her gently on the couch to watch the game.

Jess watched eagerly. She didn't know who any of the players were after nearly eight years of solitude, but she didn't care. It was still the same game. Her dad was diligent on the remote control and made sure she didn't see one single commercial or hear anything that wasn't related to their game, though Anger did stir within her briefly every time he would have to fast forward. It reminded her of her illness and George's refusal to believe her anytime she said anything derogatory about her past.

But then the game would come back on and anger would be silent and outer happy would make itself known.

And the Giants won 7-4.

Jess went to bed with the joyous sound of baseball ringing in her ears. With her eyes closed she could almost *smell the field. The vendors hollered on both sides of her, barking for hungry fans to buy peanuts and hot dogs, beer and soda.*

She opened her eyes and saw she was standing at the backstop behind home plate with the field spread out before her. The players were running to their positions, each coming from the dugout as their names were called by a ghostly announcer who spoke in unintelligible muffled tones.

She watched as they warmed up. The outfielders played catch in the outfield. The first baseman threw grounders at the infielders and they threw them back.

The pitcher warmed up on the mound.

His windup was fluid and he threw the ball hard and it made a loud smack when it hit the catcher's mitt.

He repeated his windup over and over and over while Jess watched from only a few feet away.

Then he threw one a little too high.

The catcher leapt, but to no avail, and the ball sailed over his head, rolling toward Jess until it stopped just inches from her feet.

He approached her to retrieve the ball. "Hi, Jess."

Jess looked into silvery-blue eyes and her heart raced. "Brody?"

He took off his mask. "Yes, Baby. I'm here. It's been so long."

"Oh, God, Brody, how can this be?" Jess cried freely, and her Happy ballooned up and over and squashed Angry flat. Real Happy. Real Happy beat outside happy any day of the week.

"It can be because it is, Jess."

His fingers caressed her cheek as she closed her eyes and reached up to take his hand in hers, but it wasn't there. She only touched her own damp skin. "Where are you?"

"I'm still here, Jess."

She opened her eyes. He was perfect even through her tears. "Why can't I feel you?"

"You feel me in your heart, and that's enough for now."

"No!" Jess began to sob. "No, it's NOT enough! Brody, everything is wrong without you. Nobody believes me. Nobody understands me. I'm so unhappy. I need you."

"I need you, too."

Jess almost choked on her tears as Brody and the ball field began to fade away. "Where are you going? Come back!"

"I love you, Jess Waterford." His voice moved from in front of her to within her.
Come back.
But he didn't come back.
And Real Happy left with him.

The sun barely peeked over the mountains as Jess rose slowly and went to the bathroom to wash the tears from her face. Two more orange and white pills had been placed in the annoyingly cheerful pink and purple butterfly dish on her sink.

She pulled a towel down from the rack and dried her face, and then she took in a deep breath and did something she hadn't done in a long time. She braced herself with one hand on either side of the sink, and faced the mirror full on. Her image looked back at her with her mother's reflection and churned her stomach.

Bitch.

After dreaming about Brody, she'd hoped she would be what she had been in her imaginary world: mousy brown hair, flush and full cheeks, kind hazel-green eyes. Instead she stared at the spitting image of her mother: the eyes of searing gray that had glared through a puff of smoke, the flaming red hair that swirled around her when she'd swing a fist, the thin pink lips that blamed her incessantly for ruining her career and her body, and in return, ruined her daughter's mind and spirit.

She had stopped talking to George about her mother and he was still hell bent on reminding her she was jealous. Jealous of her mother's beauty and her hunger for her father's affection even though at this moment in time, she *had* her mother's looks and her father's full attention. It didn't matter. It was all Jess's fault. It was all about her own insecurities. Her own flaws. Her own inadequacies. So she made someone up that would make her feel beautiful and give her the attention she thought she deserved.

Brody.

The one person who believed her. The one person she missed the most. The one person who wasn't really a person at all.

Jess looked down again at the medicine in the dish. Two oblong orange and white capsules.

If only taking one pill helped her see Brody, she could risk it again, right? She could try it again, and if she felt any differently—if her anger bubbled too hot, if she couldn't handle it—she could always go back to two.

She went back to the memory of her dad and the cost of the medicine. It wasn't as if she had to chuck it down the toilet and waste it. She could just hide it away somewhere and secretly put it back in the bottle when he wasn't looking. Her eyes darted around the bathroom for something she could conceal the pill in. She filtered through shelves, the medicine cabinet, and beneath the sink.

Somewhere her dad wouldn't look if he became suspicious.

She laughed to herself when she saw the tampon box. He certainly wouldn't look there. Even though he had had to buy them for her, he would never remove them from the plastic bag, and always handed them to her, his arm at full length as if he had to keep it as far away from his body so the vile package within wouldn't get girly-bugs on him.

Her more rational self knew she shouldn't do it. Not only did she not want to upset her father, but she also feared what George would say to her if he found out. Then something else inside her told her George wouldn't even believe she had the nerve to stop taking her medication. He wouldn't believe her even if she told him.

How she longed for someone who would believe her.

She dropped one capsule into the tampon box and it landed with a hollow *thonk* when it met the cardboard bottom. She replaced the box beneath the sink, downed the other pill, and practiced her outer happy.

KIM HARNES

Chapter Twenty-Seven

"George said you did well in your session yesterday." Wesley smiled across the kitchen table over his dinner. "And this meatloaf is outstanding!"

Jess grinned back at her dad. She had certainly demonstrated a knack for cooking since she'd been home. Since she wasn't allowed to watch television, she'd asked if she could read. But then the only books she was allowed to read were Dr. Seuss, the dictionary, and cookbooks. She mostly chose the latter, and decided to put her time and new knowledge to good use. George had initially voiced his concern over her use of sharp utensils, but Jess argued it was relaxing and therapeutic. Her father must have apparently believed she wasn't apt to stab him in the face with a butcher knife anytime soon, and he was on the receiving end of delicious, hot meals, so he was all for the idea.

"I'll take care of these dishes, J-Bird." Wesley stood up and began to clear the table. "Why don't you go relax?"

Relax. Sure. Though she had spent the better part of the afternoon perusing Webster's, she didn't think the word "relax" was currently in her vocabulary. Relaxing was something normal people did to escape their busy lives, to slow down and think about other things. That wasn't something Jess thought was productive to do in her current situation, as slowing down only allowed her to stew over what was wrong within her and made more kindling for her Anger. She maintained the outer charade and smiled back at her dad, anyway. "Thanks."

She excused herself from the table, and slowly made her way down the short hallway to change into her pajamas and brush her teeth. The sound of the kitchen faucet and clanking dishes diminished with each step, and almost disappeared when she turned the corner and caught her reflection in the bathroom mirror.

"Bitch."

It made her feel good to say it out loud. Not to herself, of course, but to her mother, as she always deemed it to be her reflection and not Jess's she saw. Avoiding the opposing face as much as possible, she began to brush her teeth and think about Brody. The way he looked. The way he sauntered to class and the way he was so incredible at baseball. The way he would always know what to say when she was down, and the way he would always listen when she needed him to. And the way he would kiss her.

"Are you okay in here?"

Jess jumped. She'd been too involved in her own thoughts to hear when her father had turned off the faucet, started the dish washer, and made his way down the hall. "Yeah. Just brushing my teeth."

"Well, hurry up. There's another game on tonight. And don't forget to take your medicine." He motioned to the ceramic dish that still held two capsules.

A quick spark of Anger clouded her senses. Even though she'd recently reduced her dosage, didn't she *always* remember to take her medicine? Was there *ever* a day her father went to refill the dish and it wasn't empty? She gritted her teeth against the vile things she wanted to say. "I won't forget."

Wesley turned to leave and Jess closed the door behind him. After she had put her toothbrush away, she retrieved the tampon box from beneath the sink, dropped one pill in with a satisfying *plonk*, and then washed the other down with a quick swig from the tap. She changed into her pajamas, and joined her father on the couch, feeling less Irritation toward him at the prospect of being able to watch baseball. The Giants had already played four innings, but Wesley was able to start it over from the beginning.

"That amazes me." Jess stared at the remote in her dad's hand.

"What's that?"

"Well, it used to be if we missed half the game, we just missed half the game."

Wesley grinned. "Ah, yes. The joys of DVR."

"Hell of an invention."

He chuckled. "Yes. Yes, it is."

After the first inning, though Jess wanted to keep watching, she couldn't help but think that if she were asleep she'd get to be with Brody. She longed to see him again, and hoped he'd be in her dreams. She yearned to have the best of both worlds and be able to maintain on the outside, and still have Brody at night. Even if she couldn't hold him, she wanted to be near him. To look at him. To tell him about her problems. The real ones, and not what she told George.

When the last inning was over and the Giants lost, Jess nearly jumped off the couch and hurried to her room.

"J-Bird?" Her dad entered and sat at the edge of her bed. "It's just a game. They'll win tomorrow." He ruffled the hair on her forehead.

Jess thought it amusing her father took her eagerness to go to bed as being upset over the loss. "I know, Dad." Any excuse her father concocted was better than having to tell him why she really wanted to sleep.

"Night, Jess."

She watched her dad leave the room, and then she closed her eyes tightly and waited for sleep to come.

And waited.

And waited.

So eager to see Brody, her body refused to shut itself down. Midnight came and went. One o'clock came and went. Her dad's soft snores reverberated from across the hall and twirled Angry like a wicked game of Spin the Bottle and it pointed at her father for the second time that day. Why was he able to sleep when she couldn't? That wasn't fair. Two o'clock came and went.

Why couldn't she just go to sleep?

Why couldn't she just *let the darkness of the night overtake her and all that was left was a lamppost shining down on wet blacktop. A figure moved silently through the shadows until the lamplight spilled across his face and reflected in his eyes. Tall. Handsome. Perfect. Brody.*

Jess's heart beat solidly against her chest and tears fell openly as he approached her. He smiled as he slowly raised his hand and touched her face. "You did it, Jess." She closed her eyes as he wiped a tear from her cheek with his thumb and then threaded his hand through the hair at the nape of her neck. It was exquisite.

She reached out toward him and when she felt his chest against her palm she cried harder. His heart beat in time with hers. "I can touch you."

"And it can only get better."

She tilted her head upward and allowed his lips to press against her own. Firm, solid, real. Or, at least, real enough.

She never wanted to awaken.

"You've done well, Jess." Brody looked into her eyes and smiled. "You're bringing me back. I've wanted to kiss you like that for so long."

Jess smiled back. She loved to hear when she'd done something well. "I can handle it, Brody. I think I can handle just taking one pill. I know I can."

Brody returned her smile. "I bet you could handle taking none at all."

Jess shuddered. None at all? "Baby, I don't know." She contemplated the odds. The risk of doing that could be disastrous. Then she looked back into Brody's face and her pulse quickened. But oh, what she would gain.

"The medicine, Jess. Remember what it did to me before?" He pulled a pine needle out from the seat of his jeans and Jess was mildly amused at the memory, but quickly became horror-stricken as it morphed into a syringe. "Remember how it made me so sick in the clearing?" He backed away from her and reached his hand to his temple. "Remember the pain?" He continued to step backward and Jess's anguish enveloped her. "Do you remember?" Brody's nose began to bleed. It dribbled down his chin and caked his white t-shirt. "Remember the blood?" He stretched out his ooze-covered hand toward Jess. Huge drops burned scarlet in the lamplight and disappeared as they hit the blacktop. "Remember?" He began to fade and Jess began to sob.

"My God, Brody, NO!"

"I need you to remember, Jess." His voice weakened as his silhouette grew fainter.

"NO, BRODY, NO! COME BACK!"

"Remember." Merely a whisper inside her mind.

"I'll remember, Brody."

"You won't remember a thing." As Brody's image disappeared completely, the pudgy, pock marked orderly appeared in his place, his breath not sweet this time, but reeking of rotten salami and sour mustard and it *overpowered her as he leaned in to kiss her. "You won't remember a thing."*

She turned away from him, disgusted.

"She's remembering a lot, Wesley."

The orderly disappeared and Jess pivoted toward the new voice. George's voice. He was sitting casually behind his desk, though not in his office. They were still on the blacktop and the lamplight spilled atop his bushy, white eyebrows casting eerie shadows across his face.

Her father leaned forward in his chair. "Do you think she'll eventually figure everything out?"

"Oh, I think it's only a matter of time."

"Well, what do you think we should do about it?"

George chuckled. "What does it really matter?"

"Why are you being so nonchalant?"

George's chuckle escalated to snickering. "Well, because, really ... who's going to believe her, anyway?" Snickering escalated to peals of sick laughter that bounced off walls that didn't exist.

Wesley joined suit. "You've got a point, there, don't you?"

Anger flourished within her as they laughed together at her expense.

Mocking her.

Ridiculing her.

Their laughter turned to beeping and she spun again.

The blacktop and George's desk melted away and she stood at the foot of her father's bed seething with Anger as he rolled over and tapped the snooze on his alarm clock.

The beeping ceased.

The Anger didn't.

Chapter Twenty-Eight

Jess stared at her father with pure Hatred simmering within her. She wanted to hurt him. To make him pay for what he'd said. For how he'd laughed. For how they'd both laughed.

But, yet, they really hadn't, had they?

It had all been just a dream. But how had she made it to the foot of his bed? She knew she was no longer asleep, yet the emotion carried over with her; the pure Fury that pulsed within her like molten lava.

Disgust and Guilt over how she'd just felt toward her father quickly overpowered Anger. It nauseated her and bile burned the back of her throat. She was frozen in place with Fear and was thankful she had nothing in her stomach to vomit. Tears erupted from her eyes.

Wesley awoke and looked at his daughter. "J-Bird?" He sat up, obviously alarmed. "J-Bird, are you okay?"

Jess didn't know what to do or say.

"Did you have a bad dream?"

You need to react here, Jess. Brody's voice whispered inside her head. *Answer him.* Bad dream? Yes. That sounded right. Jess nodded stiffly. "Yes, Daddy. Bad dream."

"Well, come here and let Daddy make it better." Jess realized she needed his comfort and thankfully her mind allowed her body to move toward him and be enveloped in his outstretched arms.

She continued to weep. "What's wrong with me?"

Wesley stroked her hair. "Bad dreams are normal, Jess. They happen. You're okay."

His voice and his words soothed her.

It wasn't because she'd thrown a few pills into the blue cardboard box beneath her bathroom sink. Bad dreams were normal. She was normal.

She tucked Anger away in Its place and allowed her father to console her.

When she stopped crying, her dad sat up. "How'd you like me to fix you some breakfast?"

Jess grinned. "What do you plan to burn for me this morning?"

Wesley bowed his head in faux defeat. "Alas, sadly, my dear, unless you prefer crunchy scrambled eggs and burnt toast, it will be cereal or nothing."

Jess scrunched her nose. "I'm pretty sure I'd rather have nothing."

His head bowed lower.

"But I bet cooking breakfast for you will make *me* feel a lot better."

He raised his head and lifted his hands in triumph. "Aha! My evil plan worked!"

Jess smiled and followed after her dad who was hopping comically down the hallway toward the kitchen.

Fifteen minutes later Wesley dipped toast into eggs over easy with one hand and shoved bacon into his mouth with the other. "This is so much better than cereal. Thanks, J-Bird."

"You're very welcome." She stood and rinsed off her own plate in the sink and placed it in the dishwasher. "Same time at George's today?"

"Yup." His mouth was still mostly full.

"I'll go get ready."

Jess walked into the bathroom and looked in the mirror. "Bitch." She was doing that a lot lately. Every time she saw her reflection, to be precise. It was so easy to pretend it wasn't herself she saw in the glass, and gratifying to shoot some of her Anger toward her mother with no fear of retaliation.

Her mother stared back, silent as usual.

Jess looked at the orange and white duo in the ceramic dish as Brody's voice echoed in her ears. *I bet you could handle taking none at all.*

None.

Jess shuddered against the chill that seeped its way up her spine.

She remembered what the medication had done to Brody. Just like he'd said to remember. The pain. The blood.

She reached for the box beneath the sink.

Plunk. Plunk.

Good girl.

How she loved to be complimented.

****

Jess darted through the hallways of the hospital quickly, her dad almost having to run to keep up.

"What's going on, J-Bird?" He was huffing, out of breath.

Jess wanted the orderly.

She thought there had to have been some significance in the fact that his face intruded on her dream the night before and tried to kiss her. Something inside her that said maybe if she could smell his scent— Brody's scent—she'd have an actual, real-life connection to her dreams. A solid reminder to his imaginary form.

But she couldn't find him anywhere.

She took another lap around the hospital, her dad hot on her heels.

"Slow down, J-Bird! Come on!"

Jess made it to George's office door for the third time around and finally gave up. "He's not here." Disappointment rose above Anger, but only just barely.

Her dad reached her, stopped, and bent over gasping, his hands on his knees. "Who's not here? What are you talking about?" Wesley stood upright slowly, his hand moving to the stitch in his side.

"Nobody." Defeated, Jess opened the office door and walked in.

"You're late," George accused her as she sat down.

"We were here on time." Wesley was quick to defend himself and throw Jess under the bus. "Jess decided to make three rounds through the building looking for nobody." He said the last word like it left a bad taste in his mouth.

Snitch.

The scarred, bushy tuft of hair over George's left eye rose and crinkled his brow as he turned his head and cocked it toward Jess. "Looking for nobody?" He picked up his pen and made the writing tip snap outward with a curt flick of his thumb. "Whom were you looking for, Jess?"

"Whom? Someone whom works here, that's whom." She realized her mistake the moment she spoke the words. *Breathe in, breathe out, Jess*, she reminded herself. *Don't get Angry. Or, at least, don't let them see it.*

Scribble-scribble.

"Sorry." She sat back in her chair.

"I accept your apology." He cocked his head to the other side. "But I'd also still like the truth."

The truth, Jess thought contemptuously. Yes, *that* was what George was interested in. The truth. She guessed it didn't matter about the "whom" so much as the "why" in this case, anyway, so she let spill. "I was looking for the orderly who said goodbye to me the night before I left."

"You mean Hal? And why were you looking for him?"

Of *course* he'd ask the "why." Jerk. "Because he was nice to me. And because he wanted to know about my recuperation." Why the hell not? "And because he smelled good."

George looked down at his notepad as if the words that were scrawled on the page were foreign to him even though he'd been the one to write them. "What did he smell like?"

Jess grinned. *Brody.* "Mustard."

George looked as though he were trying to suppress a laugh. "Mustard?"

"And cologne sometimes." *Brody's cologne.* "But mostly it was just something with mustard."

"I don't ever remember his wearing cologne."

Brody's voice entered her mind and goose bumps pimpled her flesh. *He only wore cologne on date nights.*

George continued. "But that's neither here nor there. I'm sorry to inform you, Jess, but Hal no longer works here."

"He … he doesn't? Why not?" Jess's plan was all for naught, and Sadness roused within her stomach.

"He's been discharged."

"Discharged as in fired? Why?" How could they fire him? Didn't they know she'd need him? What had he done?

Unspeakable things. Things he should be ashamed of.

Her mind whirred with the possibilities of what led to his release. Was he an alcoholic? A drug addict? Did he beat his patients? Or, worse than that, did he molest them?

Ding ding ding ... we have a winner. Brody's voice inside Jess's mind was sarcastic, but sympathetic.

Jess went rigid. What if that were true? Pieces of both of her real and make-believe worlds had collided before. What if what Brody had done to her willingly in her imagination, the orderly had done simultaneously for real and without permission?

It couldn't have been.

It makes sense.

Jess looked at her hands. It did make sense. It actually made perfect sense. As they drove home, as she mindlessly cooked dinner, and as she lay in bed that night, she continuously replayed their last encounter over and over in her mind.

"Do ... do you remember anything? Like ... from when you were out of it?"

Now, why would he have asked that? It didn't occur to her to be an odd question at the time, but it certainly was now. Why would he need to know if she could remember unless he'd been doing something he shouldn't have?

George was wrong. She didn't know about sex because of her hormones or her animal instincts or her changing body.

She knew about sex because she'd had sex. With Brody in her mind, and the orderly in her room.

Overpowering feelings, jumbled until they were unrecognizable, washed over her like waves against the shore. Over and over they crashed against her, confirming within her what had taken place in her hospital room.

Validating her suspicions. What he'd done to her. What he had probably done to countless others as well.

But he was gone now. He couldn't do that anymore.

And Jess didn't need him or his reminder of Brody, because she would see Brody on her own soon enough.

Jess pulled the covers up to her neck and thought of two new orange and white capsules in a blue tampon box in the dark cupboard beneath her sink.

Soon enough.

KIM HARNES

Chapter Twenty-Nine

Baseball season ended, the leaves changed and fell, the snow covered them up and then melted, new leaves grew back and Spring Training began again. Another birthday had come and gone. Jess's medication no longer thwacked hollowly into the bottom of the blue tampon box, but now landed on a soft pillow of orange and white capsules.

For the most part, she'd been fine. Anger continued to be a constant. On several more occasions she'd awakened at the foot of her father's bed, usually with the same sense of Fury roiling within her, but it always settled when he'd wake up, hug her, and let her fix his breakfast.

She'd presented him with her idea about the orderly, and he seemed to accept her hypothesis, but then the subject was dismissed never to be brought up again.

When she dreamed of Brody, he told her not to mention the theory to George, so she hadn't. And she dreamed of Brody every night. He was also speaking inside her mind more and more while she was awake. At first she wondered if she should be concerned, but after awhile she resigned herself to the fact that seeing Brody was what she wanted, anyway, so hearing his voice in her head was merely a case of sweet serendipity.

So everything in her life was normal.

Day in, day out. Normal.

Until one blustery day when Brody's voice inside her head asked why her dad always detoured around the old little league ballpark.

I don't know, Jess thought to Brody. *That's a good question. Maybe you should ask him.*

And as they drove home from her latest and greatest session with George, she did just that.

He seemed as though he didn't want to answer. "Why do you want to know?"

"Curiosity, I guess." *Curiosity and my boyfriend.*

"It's … I'm not sure George would approve."

"Well, why not?" Jess looked up at the darkening sky. It was only just after five, but early spring days were still short.

Wesley appeared to mull the idea over. It was almost painful to watch. "I guess I can. I'm just afraid it will be … unsettling to you."

"Why would it be unsettling?" Jess perked up at the possibility she was going to get her way. "That was my most favorite place in the world when I was … before."

Wesley looked at her, his face flush with worry. Then he turned the car around and headed toward the park. "If there's a game going on, we are just driving by."

"Deal."

But when they arrived, the field was dark. Wesley pulled into the parking lot, the asphalt crunching beneath the tires and Jess, wide-eyed with anticipation, realized something that almost made her scream out loud. Though Fear coursed through her, she calmly spoke to her father. "Stop the car, please, Dad."

Wesley did and Jess exited slowly. She walked over to the rear of the snack bar and stopped alongside the brick building that was lit only by a lamppost in the middle of the blacktop.

No wonder her dad hadn't wanted to bring her here.

This was where she'd killed her mother.

She remembered.

Her parents had left the game right after she'd scored her first inside-the-park homerun. She had expected her dad to come back for her, but she waited and waited and waited in the pouring rain and lightning.

Then her mother had shown up instead.

Jess was frozen in place.

"Listen, you little shit. Either you get in this car, or I drive off without you and consider you a runaway. No skin off my ass either way."

And still, Jess could not move.

The car door opened and Amanda flicked her cigarette onto the pavement. It made a hiss as the rain extinguished the ember at the tip. "Get in the car, you disgusting little troll!" She had reached Jess in two giant steps with her long legs and dug her French manicure into the flesh on her shoulders as she wrestled her toward the car.

Jess's duffel bag dragged along behind her and it made a sick sound as it slid across the wet asphalt.

"Hurry up!"

Her mother's foot hit her square in her lower back knocking her to the ground and causing her head to hit the open car door.

Brody was beside her then. Thankfully. Blessedly. "Your bat."

"My ... my what?"

"Your bat, Jess. Get your bat out of your duffel bag. It's the only way."

Jess scrambled over to her bag as her mother's foot made contact again, this time hitting Jess right between the shoulder blades and sending her face first into the pavement. Fresh blood mingled with the rain and dripped down her nose and chin. She unzipped the bag and fumbled around, blindly searching for the hilt of her bat.

"I'm getting wet, you stupid shit!" Jess's mom kicked again striking Jess hard in the upper thigh. "Don't make me kill you. I've got too much invested in you to kill you now."

Jess's hands still reached in vain for the handle of her Louisville Slugger.

"All those times I had to sleep with that saggy-balled white-haired old man so he'd believe me instead of you. All those times I let those liver spotted, wrinkled old hands touch my body so he would think you were the liar."

Jess smelled vodka strong and stale on her mother's breath.

"All those times I've lied to your father and told him this baby is his so he wouldn't know it was George's instead."

Jess was still on her back on the wet pavement, her fingers unsuccessfully groping for their prize. Amanda lifted her foot just above Jess's face and made ready to stomp the spiked heel into her right eye. "All those times I only slapped you when I really wanted to send you back to hell where you belong." The foot came down. "Well, welcome to hell, Jessica!"

It was wet and slippery, but Jess took the bat in both hands and rolled away from her mother's foot. She jumped up and swung with all her might just as lightning flashed across the sky illuminating Amanda Waterford's shocked expression. The immediate thunder mostly drowned the screams and Jess didn't know if they were hers or her mother's. Again and again Jess swung until there was no longer the solid crunch of bat on skull, but the softer thud of a golf club in a sand trap.

Jess dropped the bat. She collapsed to the ground and sobbed, both hands over her face, both legs beneath her, the dim light of the lamppost cascading softly over her delicate frame.

"This is what I was afraid of."

Jess forgot her father had been there and flinched away from him at first, but he wrapped his arms around her tightly.

"I know you're sorry, Jess. I know you didn't mean to."

Sorry? He thought she was sorry? Anger twisted her insides. "Take me home."

They were both silent as they pulled into the apartment complex. "Why don't you go get ready for bed and take your medicine? I'll be in to kiss you goodnight in a little bit."

Jess slowly climbed the stairs and let herself into the apartment. She wanted nothing more than to wash off the day. To let the hot water rinse the stink of her mother down the drain. She wanted to bask in her vindication, and couldn't wait to fall asleep and have someone to join her in believing her Anger was righteous Anger. "Bitch." Jess continued her routine as she passed the bathroom mirror. She reached for the tampon box and dropped her pills in.

"Who are you calling a bitch?"

Jess wasn't expecting her reflection to speak back, but she stared deeply into the gray eyes that stared deeply back into hers. "I'm calling *you* a bitch, *Mother.*"

"Let's ask the question of who killed who, here, shall we?" As her mother taunted her from the other side of the mirror, tendrils of smoke escaped her mouth and licked the back of the glass.

Jess stood strong. The Anger coursed through her and gave her power she didn't know she had. "Let's first ask the question of why."

"Why? Well, I'm sure I don't know why. I was a good mother."

Jess snorted. "A good mother? Good mother's don't beat their children and have affairs to cover it up."

"I gave you everything you ever wanted." Blood began to trickle down the left side of her mother's head. "Just ask George and your father."

"They'll tell me what you've coerced them to tell me. What you've brainwashed them to believe about you."

A red trail oozed thick down her mother's cheek and dripped onto her shoulder as she began to shriek her accusations. "You stole my youth and you wrecked my body and then you took my life." Jess watched the mirror as the blood continued to dribble and then pour from the open wound in her mother's temple. It gushed down her face and pasted her clothes to her body. "I cared for you and fed you and nurtured you." She began to turn ashen as she rapidly decomposed. Her skin sunk into hollow cheeks as she deteriorated. Her voice now came out as a hiss through shriveled lips. "You did this to me."

Jess glared back at her mother with no remorse. Only Anger. "You did *this* to *me* first."

The loud rap on the door made Jess jump and when she looked back at the mirror, her reflection was her own again—till mostly mom-like, but hers just the same.

"What are you doing in there, J-Bird? Are you talking to someone?" Her father's voice sounded troubled. Worried.

Jess thought quickly and opened the door. "I was just remembering an old song we used to sing when I was a kid."

He looked relieved. "What song is that?"

Jess grinned an evil grin. "The Old Gray Mare."

"She ain't what she used to be." Wesley smiled at his daughter.

Jess looked back at the mirror. "No, she sure ain't."

KIM HARNES

Chapter Thirty

"You told me to do it. You told me to get the bat and kill my own mother."

"It was the only way, Jess. She'd have killed you first if you hadn't reacted. If she'd have killed you, we'd never have gotten to be together." He brushed a lock of hair off her forehead. *"And you were never truly happy until she was gone from your life."*

"But I killed her. She was awful and unloving, but I killed her. And her baby."

"George's baby." His words were harsh, but true, and Anger shot through Jess like a bolt of lightning. Brody squeezed her tighter. *"It killed my mother, too. Remember?"*

"It did?"

"Yes, Jess. We're one and the same, Baby."

Jess thought back and realized what he'd said was true. Brody's mother was everything she'd wanted her mother to be, but everything her mother really wasn't. And when Amanda had made her disappearing act in Jess's mind, Brody's mother had died as well. "I'm sorry, Brody."

"Don't be sorry, Jess. You needed it to be that way. That's what brought us closer. We had both lost our mothers and we had that in common. That and baseball. And nothing was going to tear us apart. And nothing will again. I'll see to that." He kissed the tip of her nose. *"I love you, Jess."*

"I love you, too, Brody."

"It's time to wake up now."

Jess tried to squish her eyelids together tighter so she could go back to sleep and dream, but she knew it was a lost cause. She threw off the covers and slumped to the kitchen to make breakfast.

Her father met her at the table. "George wants to see you today."

Jess protested. "But today's my day off!"

"I know." He rubbed the worry off his forehead. "It's my fault. It's about last night. He wants to talk to you about the ballpark."

"Damn it, Dad!"

"Jessica!"

Fury flashed across her face at the mention of her full name, but her voice stayed calm and steady. "Jess."

"I'm sorry, Jess. But please don't curse at me."

"Curse at you? Dad, I'm an eighteen-year-old who was convicted of murder at the age of nine. I think cursing is a bit below my echelon of delinquency."

Though he cringed slightly at the imagery, Wesley laughed a tired laugh. "You really should stop reading the dictionary."

"Buy me more cook books." She slid an omelet onto her father's plate, smiled, and kissed the top of his head.

"I really am sorry."

"Me, too." Lie or not, he appeared to have appreciated the gesture.

She had a few things she wanted to discuss with George, anyway.

****

"Your father tells me you asked to go to the scene of the crime." Real or imagined, George seemed smug. Arrogant.

"Well, I didn't know it was the scene of the crime at the time." Jess returned his attitude with some haughtiness of her own.

"You get him, Jess."

Jess spun toward the familiar voice. Brody sat on the floor beneath the photograph of a butterfly emerging from a cocoon on George's wall. He looked weak, but solid, and Jess's heart leapt out of her chest.

"Jess?" George's presence was now merely a distraction to her. She had Brody.

"What?"

"So, what happened when you got to the ballpark?"

Jess looked to Brody for direction.

"You can tell him."

Jess proceeded to tell George the story of how she'd realized where she was, and how she'd remembered what happened, and how she remembered what her mother had said to her.

"And what did she say?" George was too pompous to be fearful.

Jess looked at Brody again and he blew her a kiss. Her Confidence soared. "She said a lot of interesting things about you, George."

"About me?" His tone held false disbelief.

"Yes. You and your saggy balls."

Brody laughed out loud. His sweet, dulcet laugh.

George wasn't amused. "My … saggy balls, you say? Anything else?"

"Yes, and please feel free to write all this down." Jess noted George was missing his usual pad of paper and pen. "Right before I killed her she told me she hated having your gross old body pressed against hers but she knew she had to so she could save her own tight, supple little ass." Well, it wasn't exactly verbatim. But it was close enough.

George seethed. Jess was enjoying herself.

"She said she used to hump you to keep you submissive. I guess it worked."

"ENOUGH!" George slammed his hand down on the desk.

Jess was shocked at first at George's outburst, but grinned when she noticed Brody trying to say something. He was laughing so hard he could barely catch his breath, and finally managed to squeak out, "H–humping…s–s–saggy b–balls!" Peals of laughter bounced of the photographs in George's office and back to Jess, amplifying her Courage.

She smiled coyly at George and bit her bottom lip.

"I don't EVER want to hear you say that again. NONE of it is factual, you have no proof of any of it, and you're only taking steps backward in your recovery."

Jess sprang back, wounded. "But … but it's true, George."

"Of course it's not true. It's just another figment of your imagination. Another story made up to improve your situation."

Jess deflated. Where she had wanted to injure George—to let him know she knew what he'd done to her—he had turned it back around and made it about her crazies.

And Brody wasn't laughing anymore.

It didn't matter. No matter what she said or did, no one would ever believe her.

"I believe you, Jess." Brody stood feebly, moved to her side, and took her hand.

Brody always believed her. When no one else would.

Despite her efforts to hold them all back, a single tear escaped and trickled down her cheek.

"Why are you crying, Jess?" George's new tone only seemed to mock her pain.

"You're no better than she was." It was an unkind statement, but it was a true one. He had helped in her downward spiral toward insanity. He had been a co-conspirator. An ally of the most wicked villain of all.

Her mother.

Jess simmered in her Anger and for the rest of the session she said nothing. She sat there and glared at George, Livid over his bogus victory.

The ride home wasn't much better.

Her only comfort was that Brody was with her. Yes, weak and untouchable now, but a couple more pills in a tampon box, and she'd be able to hold him on the outside as well as in her dreams.

"Bitch," she hissed at the bathroom mirror looking for a fight.

"You again?" Her mother exhaled a spiral of smoke that kissed the mom-side of the mirror seductively, its ethereal fingers spreading outward and upward as if summoning her to join it on its side of the glass.

"How could you do that to Dad?"

"Do what to your dad? Marry him? Dress half naked in front of him? Have sex with him? Really, Jess, if you don't know about sex by now, it's a bit late for your *mother* to tell you, isn't it?" The sarcasm dripped off her lips.

"I mean cheat on him. Get pregnant with someone else's child."

"Oh, that part was easy." Her smile would have been beautiful if there weren't so much evil behind it.

"Look at yourself, Jess. You're everything I was. Gorgeous. Sumptuous. Desirable. Men would do anything for me, just as they would for you if you weren't so ape shit crazy."

"I am NOT crazy!"

"No, of course you're not."

Jess's attempts to control her Anger were failing. "If I am, it's because you made me this way."

"Well, that was my plan all along, dear heart." The tag at the end came out as more of an insult than a term of endearment. "I hated you from the day I found out you were conceived. I had an appointment to abort you, but your idiot father found that damn test in the trash can and got all happy on me. I tried what I could to miscarry. Drank like a fish, smoked like a chimney, punched myself in the stomach when your father wasn't looking."

"You're sick."

"You're the one with the diagnosis, love." She took a drag of her cigarette and continued with her tale. "When you were done stretching the shit out of my body and finally came out, I loathed you even more. You were nothing but a parasite needing constant attention and care. Well, your father did all of it, of course. I didn't even want to touch you, and since you'd ruined my body and I couldn't model anymore, I continued to drink to feel numb. Wesley thought I had post-partum depression, the fool. And that's when he introduced me to George."

"Dad introduced you?"

"Oh, yes. And from the first moment I saw that creepy old doctor and how he looked me up and down, undressed me with his eyes, I knew I would have him eating out of the palm of my hand. I could get him to say anything I wanted him to say. And here you are as proof."

"But Dad …"

"Your father knew it, too. He knew what was going on, Jess. He just chose to be manipulated by the Queen, yours truly, Amanda Waterford. As long as I dressed in almost nothing and pleasured him often, he was my pawn. Don't you doubt it for a minute."

"Dad knew?"

"Dad knew."

"And he did nothing to stop it?" Jess felt fresh tears.

"Turn around and look at your ass. Most men would do anything for a pair of tits and a nice ass."

"I Hate you."

"Temper, temper, Jessica. Is that any way to talk to your mother?"

"My name is Jess, and my mother is dead."

****

In the wee hours of the morning, Jess awakened at the foot of her father's bed. Anger was with her, heated and furious as usual. The difference this time, though, was the bat she held in her hands.

KIM HARNES

Chapter Thirty-One

Jess was thankful her father hadn't awakened and she was able to put the bat where it belonged before he noticed it was missing. Anger, though still present, was subdued to its usual level of just below boiling.

She was also thankful to have the day to herself and not have to go anywhere or do anything or see anyone—well, the only one she was allowed to see, namely George. Much to her delight, her father had bought her a new cookbook, and she thumbed through the pages most of the day trying to figure out what she wanted to make for dinner. Brody chose hamburgers with mustard, but Jess thought she'd try something a little fancier, and she was already chopping the vegetables.

"Who were you talking to last night, J-Bird?" By the nervousness in her dad's voice, Jess figured he'd been trying to ask her this question all day, and was either avoiding the answer, or was afraid of it. "Was it … was it Brody?"

Jess looked at Brody, lying on the couch, his feet propped up on the arm, his fingers laced behind his head. "Not this time, Double-Double-U."

Jess was amused at Brody's new and completely disrespectful nickname for Wesley Waterford and she smiled. "That's just silly, Dad. You know Brody isn't real." The words came out sweet, but they burned her throat like acid. Brody made light of it, though, and pretended to stab himself in the gut with a long sword and die a dramatic death, flailing on the couch until he was finally still, sprawled comically across the cushions, his tongue lolling to one side.

Jess tried not to laugh.

"But you were talking to someone, Jess. Yelling, in fact. I heard you."

The laughter got stuck in her throat. Shit. She tried to think of an excuse and turned to Brody for help.

"Tell him you were listening to the radio."

But I'm not supposed to listen to the radio.

"Isn't getting in trouble for that better than the alternative?"

Jess turned to her father. "I'm sorry, Dad. I know I'm not supposed to, but I was listening to the radio."

"And singing along," Brody added.

"And singing along," Jess echoed.

Wesley didn't appear to believe her, but accepted it anyway. "You shouldn't listen to the radio, Jess. It's against George's orders."

"I know, Daddy. I'm sorry."

Wesley grinned and kissed her cheek. "Just like your mother. I never could stay mad at her for long, either."

Jess gripped the handle of the knife a little tighter.

Brody was by her side in a heartbeat, whispering in her ear, "You're nothing like your mother."

Her hand relaxed and she continued to make dinner.

An hour later, after Jess had to mentally stop herself from setting a place for Brody at the dinner table (he lounged on the couch pretending to drool as they ate), Wesley was leaning back in his chair and rubbing his belly. "Amazing, Jess. Just awesome."

Once again, Jess relished the compliment. "Thanks, Dad."

"That's one thing your mother never did was cook."

Lightning flashed briefly through the kitchen window just as Anger sparked through Jess. Though she appreciated the fact that was one way she was NOT like her mother, she wished he'd quit bringing her up.

"Looks like a storm's rolling in." Wesley peered through the blinds in the living room and then almost sat on Brody's head.

Brody moved quickly. "Dude, I like you and all, but that doesn't mean I'm ready to get *that* close to your derrière."

Jess snickered, but stopped abruptly as more lightning flashed reminding Jess of that fateful night in the ballpark parking lot. Jess Hated rain, and it was beginning to patter the windows.

"You scared, Baby?" Brody was instantly by her side again, his arm around her shoulder.

She let herself be consoled, but didn't let her father see her being consoled. Brody walked her to the bathroom so she could get ready for bed.

"You'll never be normal, you know?" Her mother goaded her from the other side of the mirror.

"Shut up." Jess grabbed her toothbrush from its cup.

Brody put his hand on her shoulder. "Shhh. Jess, don't get too loud or your dad will hear you."

"You'll always be a freak." Smoke repelled against her mother's side of the mirror.

Jess tried to ignore her, but she was persistent.

"You'll always be a monster."

"Just forget about her, Jess."

And that's when Jess noticed three pills in the ceramic dish instead of two. Anger joined the conversation. "What the hell is this?"

Her mother cackled behind the glass. "See, Jessica? They know about you! They know you're not normal! They know you're insane!"

"Shut up." Jess tried to cover her eyes and her ears at the same time.

"They know you're crazy crazy crazy!"

"Shut UP!" Her hands began to shake as she reached for the hair at her left temple and twisted.

Brody put his hand on her back. "Jess, shhh!"

"They all know, Jessica! Everybody knows you're a rotten, dirty, crazy killer!"

"SHUT UP!"

"Jess, NO!" Brody pleaded.

But there was no calming Jess now. Anger turned to RAGE and she picked up the repulsive butterfly, its contents spilling onto the floor, and hurled it toward her mother, shattering the mirror. Dozens of silver splinters speckled the sink.

Amanda Waterford continued to screech laughter through jagged shards of broken glass.

"What's going on in here?" Wesley had thrown open the bathroom door to discover the mess within. "Jess?"

RAGE was still with her. "Why are there three pills today?"

"Jess, please." Her father reached out for her but she wouldn't be comforted. Not this time.

"Why are there three pills?"

"George was concerned, Jess. I was concerned."

"Concerned?" Though FURY swirled within her she spoke calmly.

"Yes, J-Bird. You've been talking to yourself and getting upset easier and saying off the wall things about orderlies and affairs and twirling your hair like you used to and we just didn't know what else to do. George thought we should try to increase your medication and see if that helped."

"Oh, George *thought*, did he? Well, do you know what you can tell George about his pills?" Jess reached for the box below the sink, held it to her father at eye-level, and dumped it over. Hundreds of orange and white capsules spattered the floor. "You can tell him I don't need his fucking pills."

"Oh, Jess. Oh, no, Jess." Her father looked crushed, but Jess didn't care. She stomped past him, the pill casings crunching beneath her bare feet and spewing the white powder within across the tile. "Jess, please."

She could no longer hear him, though. FURY was freight-train-loud in her ears.

But she could hear Brody. "You know what to do."

Jess went for the bat. It was right where she'd left it that morning.

Blind RAGE sent her to her father's room. She assumed it was George on the other end of the phone in his hand, and that only fueled her ANGER. "Hang up." Lightning flashed outside and the power bumped black for just a second. The rain pounded harder.

"Jess, listen to me."

"I'm done listening to you. Now you're going to listen to me."

Wesley's eyes darted quickly to the bat, and then back at Jess. "Okay. I'll listen."

"Oh, now you'll listen?" Jess spun the bat skillfully in her nimble hands.

"Yes, yes. I'll listen."

Jess felt POWER watching her dad cringe. Watching him cower between his bed and the wall – the way she had cowered during her mother's episodes. The episodes he knew of but did nothing about. Helpless. Pathetic. "Hang up."

"Please, Jess. Let George help you."

"Fuck George. Hang up."

Brody laughed beside Jess. "Why shouldn't he fuck George? Might as well keep it in the family." He seemed amused by the show.

Wesley set the phone down and put both hands in front of him. "Jess, can't we just talk?"

"I'll do the talking." The power bumped again.

Wesley just blinked, eyes wide, hands shaking.

Now that she had her father's full attention, she didn't know where to start.

"Start from the beginning," Brody coaxed from beside her.

Jess nodded. "I HATED my mother." Her right hand still on the bat, her left found the locks at her temple and twisted as she told her story.

Wesley listened quietly, seeming to want to interject, but apparently deciding that wasn't a good idea.

Brody reminded her about parts she'd forgotten and helped her stay on track with the tale. She described the abuse and the alcohol and his dismissal of it, the affair and George's cover up, Hal the orderly and her suspicion and reasoning behind it, and the baby and its real father, about how he'd wanted her to be a pitcher, but all she'd really wanted to do was catch.

Lightning flashed periodically, and the power hiccupped a few more times.

And when she was finished, she was back to just Angry and felt much better. Like a giant weight was finally lifted off her chest.

It didn't last long.

"You're sick, J-Bird."

That was all it took to send Angry back to FURY AND HELL FIRE. "I'm not sick! Why won't you believe me?"

"Because you need to take your pills, Baby Girl. You need them to get better."

"You didn't believe me even when I WAS taking my pills! Why would you start now?"

Wesley backed away, seemingly sensing Jess's ANGER and lifted his hand defensively as she choked up on the bat.

"I believe you, J-Bird. I do."

"Liar."

The power went out for good this time and Wesley never saw it coming when Jess swung for the fence.

Left temple. Right on the sweet spot.

KIM HARNES

Chapter Thirty-Two

Jess looked down at her crimson-spattered pajamas. She waited for Regret, but it didn't come. Her heavy feet carried her to the bathroom to wash the gore from her face.

Her mother's image still violated the back side of the mirror. "Nice job, Jessica." Amanda, her head wound seeping with ooze, exhaled a plume of gray poison. "Got us both now, didn't you?"

Ringlets of smoke, no longer inhibited by the solid glass, seeped through the cracks in the mirror and reached for Jess. She swiped at them with one blood-covered paw, turned on the sink, and reached for the soap. Stray orange and white capsules, now free of their blue cardboard prison, spiraled down the drain with foamy pink water.

She looked into the mirror and saw FEAR in her mother's eyes.

Emotion didn't exist within her, but rather, it *was* her, and she was unable to control it. WRATH was her name now. And WRATH had unfinished business. WRATH wasn't satisfied with a stand-up double. WRATH wanted to round third.

WRATH picked up the bat and left the apartment.

Rain poured down diluting the remaining remnants of her mayhem and causing them to dribble gruesome runners down her face. The bat dragged behind her, creating the melodic scrape of aluminum against asphalt. For some reason, notwithstanding the late hour, she knew where he'd be, and she knew the way to the hospital despite the absence of streetlights. She'd traveled it enough over the last year. Enough to have done it blindfolded.

Lightning still flashed periodically, but further off in the distance. Thunder followed, but at greater intervals and with less force. The business end of her Louisville Slugger clanked loudly against the hospital steps as she ascended. George was near. WRATH sensed his anticipation.

She walked down the hall to his door.

"Welcome, Jessica." His pompous attitude did little to subdue WRATH, and only made her hotter.

"Jess." WRATH's voice was thick. Menacing.

"Fine. Jess. Do you have any idea why you don't like the name Jessica?"

"Hmmm. I'm guessing because that's what my mother called me."

"It's what everyone in authority called you."

"Pardon?"

"I've heard your stories. I've heard your memories. Your teachers even in your imagination called you Jessica."

"My teachers in my imagination called me Jessica because your nurses called me Jessica."

George's head cocked to the side, apparently evaluating Jess's assumption. "Could be. But a nurse is technically still an authority figure, right?"

"What does it matter, anyway?" WRATH's eyes caught the assortment of photographs on George's desk. Photos of her mother half naked. Provocatively posed. WRATH Hated thong underwear. Lightning flashed feebly outside the office window and glinted upon the silver revolver that made its home next to George's pornographic album.

"Do you like my collection?"

All the sessions, all the memories and tears and bruises, everything blazed through her in a split second as Wrath went away leaving Jess behind. Vindicated. Everything she'd been through and everything she'd done was now laid out before her and she exulted in the knowledge that she was right. Years of abuse were real. Years of lies and cover-ups were real. Years of an affair were real. Years of physical and mental torture were real.

Her feelings of anger and hatred were not only real, but also warranted.

So overwhelmed with relief and heartache, she cried openly. Her grip released on the bat and it fell to the floor as she crumpled into a heap beside it.

"Why are you crying, Jessica?" George's smug, cheerful voice mocked her sorrow. "I'm still going to defend myself."

The thunder that emanated within the room was much louder than anything that could have been created from the waning storm outside, and Jess felt fire in her shoulder. A small plume of smoke escaped the end of George's gun. It reached toward her—beckoning her—and then it was gone.

Jess looked at the scarlet stain spreading rapidly across her chest. "But … but why?"

"You didn't think I was going to let you *win*, did you?" George scooped up the photographs and approached Jess, still curled on the floor, her life now pumping out of her with every beat of her heart and soaking the carpet. "Sure, as soon as you dropped your bat you really posed no threat to me, but that's not the story I'm going to tell the police when they arrive." He bent down close and whispered almost lovingly into her ear. "And, really, Jessica … even if you are still alive when they get here, it's me they're going to believe, isn't it?" Jess tried to push him away, but pain bolted through her. He stood and began to circle around her as he spoke. "You killed my lover. You killed my child." He threw photographs at Jess one by one like he was dealing a poker hand with an X-rated deck of cards. "I tried to keep you out of the picture, but you just wouldn't quit … you and your imaginary friend. How is he, by the way? Give him my regards, will you?"

Jess looked toward Brody on the floor beside her. His eyes were wide and he was clutching his own identical wound, blood seeping between his fingers. They were one and the same, after all.

George, having no more photos to throw at her, walked back to his desk and picked up his gun. He emptied the cylinder onto the writing pad, picked up one bullet, slid it into an empty chamber, slammed it shut, and spun it around.

"Now, how much of the whole story you get to hear depends upon just how lucky you are. I could end you now, or I could end you later. Either way, though, I will end you."

George cocked the gun and pulled the trigger.
Click.
George was undaunted. "Lucky you."

Jess was powerless to react as George enlightened her on his side of the story. "We had the best plan, your mother and I. After you started your little hair twirl thing—that's called Disassociation, by the way—a means of transferring your emotions to a distraction so as not to feel them. But I digress. After you began to disassociate and then conveniently started talking to your new friend Brody, your mother and I knew it would be so easy to keep our little affair going. She would bring you to my office for your sessions and I'd talk to you for a little while and pretend to be interested, and then we'd put you in a room to have craft time and make little bracelets or you'd look at my old magazines—photography for my hobby and fashion for my obsession with hot women, which explains your little imaginary career choice as well as your work hours—and your mother and I would have a half hour or more to ourselves worry free with the perfect alibi. And who but the doting mother would take so much time out of her day three days a week—sometimes more if I wanted it—to make sure her child was mentally healthy? And then you had to grow a pair and ruin it all. I knew it was self-defense the moment I saw the hospital reports of your injuries – broken ribs, contusions, and a concussion. But I paid off a few people and convinced your dad that when you'd beat your mother to death, she had merely attempted to defend herself and not the other way around. Gullible sap."

The hammer cocked again.

Click.

George grinned, apparently pleased he could continue.

Jess's vision began to blur and she laid her head down on the soft carpet. So soft. The pain in her shoulder was minimal now, and she was sure it would soon be over.

"And that sorry sap Hal. Trust fund baby. Ugly as hell and would never find a woman. So I gave him a job here and every once in a while I'd let him in with a few of the catatonic females so he could have a little touchy-feely. I kept him happy and he kept my bank account full. And then you came to and started remembering shit so I had to let him go. Another plan of mine you ruined."

Click.

Jess sank deeper into the soft floor. The weight of George's words and the promise of death pressed in on her and she closed her eyes.

George chuckled softly. "And then there was your dad. Ignorant. Pathetic. Just as much in love with your mother's body as I was. But his weakness was that he actually loved you, too. When you were comatose for so long he kept begging me to try other things. Even if they were experimental. Who knew one of them would work?"

Click.

"My, my, my. You *are* the lucky one today, aren't you, Jessica?"

Jess watched as Brody crawled over to her and held her hand. She felt almost too weak to squeeze back. "Jess, you have to get up."

But sleep was what she wanted.

"You have to end this, Jess. There are only two more left." Brody's voice was so much sweeter than George's but it was George who spoke next.

"It really is sad if you stop and think about it. The only person who loved you was your father. And judging by what I heard on the phone and what you were covered in when you got here, I'm guessing right now he's a pool of goo. Too bad you couldn't have pounded him all those years ago instead of my Amanda."

Blackness crept up on Jess.

"We're dying," Brody whispered. And it was true. She felt it. But something in George's words was keeping her there. Giving her strength. Pissing her off.

"Well, the only *real* person that loves you, I guess. Brody loves you, too. Doesn't he?"

Click.

George laughed evilly and turned toward his desk.

Brody squeezed her hand again and made eye contact with Jess. "Yes, I do."

Her heart pounded hard—either with love for Brody or her body's final attempt to cycle what little blood she had left through her veins—it didn't matter which. Brody was right. She needed to do something. She couldn't let George win this way. Not without a fight. She stretched her free hand as far as it would go until she felt cold metal against her fingertips.

"I'm almost jealous of Hal, the poor bastard. Getting to play with a hot little thing like you while you were catatonic. All of the fun and none of the yap." George still had his back to her and Jess reached further, pain shooting down her shoulder, until finally she felt the familiar foam grip in her palm.

"Yes, Jess. That's it." Brody's encouragement gave her strength she never would have thought possible. She began to pull herself off the floor. Slowly. Painfully. Warm, sticky blood trickled down her arm, gathered at her fingertips, and dripped to the floor.

"It's a shame things couldn't have been different between us, Jessica. Why, if I hadn't already had you committed, we could have had something special. You look so much like your mother."

That was the fuel she needed. Jess was gone again and her new name was VENGEANCE. And VENGEANCE was powerful.

And VENGEANCE had a bat.

George turned around, gun in hand, and pointed it toward a bloodstain on the carpet where Jess had once been.

VENGEANCE smiled.

As Brody's dad and the hospital security guard were both fond of saying ... lights out.

George's blood pattered onto the pictures of Jess's mother on the floor.

Chapter Thirty-Three

That was an awful lot of blood for just a paper cut.

When Brody had wrapped his hand in enough tissue to suppress the bleeding, Jess focused on what had caused him to bleed in the first place. She lifted the picture, one that clearly had a flaw she had somehow missed, up to her face. Blood oozed thick over the centimeter-sized block.

"Maybe we should just stop for now." Brody winced as he put pressure on the wound in his palm.

Jess looked around the den and smiled. She was home. The mirror on the wall beside the computer desk reflected mousy brown hair and hazel green eyes and her heart pounded joyfully. She knew the picture she held in her hands was about to reveal her mother's face and start her on her road to recovery. The road to misery and unhappiness and lies and cover-ups and affairs.

"You're right, Brody. We should stop. In fact, I've been thinking about giving up photography altogether."

Brody wore an impish grin. "And what will you do?"

"I was thinking of taking up cooking."

And Brody did love to eat.

Jess took one more look in the mirror and thought she saw a flash of her mother sitting on the floor in a bright white room. She had a blood-soaked bandage on her shoulder, a vacant expression, and a silly grin.

But then she was gone.

Jess snaked her arms around Brody's waist. "I love you, Brody Campbell."

"I love you, too." He pulled her closer into his body.

Jess tilted her head upward to receive his kiss. "We're going to be so happy together."

"Yes. Yes, we are."

Forever.

The End

www.kimharnes.com

Evernight Teen

www.evernightteen.com

Photo by Christian Aragon Photography

Printed in Great Britain
by Amazon

18055903R00161